MOIRS OF AN ERRANT YOUTH

Bryan Marlowe

Memoirs of an Errant Youth

Bryan Marlowe

iUniverse, Inc.
New York Lincoln Shanghai

Memoirs of an Errant Youth

Copyright © 2006 by Bryan Marlowe

iUniverse books may be ordered through booksellers or by contacting:

iUniverse
2021 Pine Lake Road, Suite 100
Lincoln, NE 68512
www.iuniverse.com
1-800-Authors (1-800-288-4677)

This book is a work of fiction. Names, characters and places are products of the author's imagination. Any resemblance is entirely coincidental.

ISBN-13: 978-0-595-38830-1 (pbk)
ISBN-13: 978-0-595-83206-4 (ebk)
ISBN-10: 0-595-38830-2 (pbk)
ISBN-10: 0-595-83206-7 (ebk)

Printed in the United States of America

CHAPTER 1

▼

World War II, as it was to be called, was all over bar the signing of a formal declaration of unconditional surrender by the Japanese. The Yanks had seen to that by dropping atomic bombs on Hiroshima and Nagasaki. Another victory celebration was on the cards, but it would not, I supposed, be as grand as the last one—VE (Victory in Europe) Day, celebrated on May 8th, when there were parties in the streets. There were hastily arranged folding chairs and trestle tables laden with food, in quantities and varieties not seen by most since before the war. Many people must have saved the ingredients for sandwiches, cakes and pies from their meagre rations to make it a day to remember—it certainly was. People sang in the streets, hugged each other, kissed and shook hands, and many young people, overjoyed by the occasion, abandoned propriety to engage in sexual activities for the first time.

For me, nearing my 16th birthday, it was a time for reflection. I had left an 'elementary' school (for students who had not passed the scholarship for admittance to a grammar school) at the age of 14, without any educational qualifications, apart from a School Leaving Certificate, which stated that I was 'good at all subjects, English showing particular promise'. Since that time I had had several jobs, none of which could be described as jobs with a future. I had worked as an assistant to a pawnbroker and jeweller, been a sort of porter-cum-stoker in a United States servicemen's club, toiled briefly as a farm labourer in Wales and as a general labourer working on the repair of war damaged houses in the much bombed London suburb of Woolwich.

I was currently employed as an apprentice compositor, a job I hated because of the tedium of setting up and dismantling galleys of type by hand. I had ambitions of becoming a reporter and had written to the *Daily Mirror* applying for a job as a copy boy. Such a job, I thought, would set me on a path that might one day lead me to a career in journalism. There were no vacancies at the time and I couldn't wait for one to arise for I needed to work to earn money to contribute to the household budget. I had been advised, by those who should have known, that a career in printing was well paid and respected, and when I was qualified I could work for a newspaper or magazine and eventually get a job as a reporter, or even a sub-editor.

The jolting of the tram as it came to its terminal stop at Southwark Bridge brought me back to reality. As I alighted, I heard a distant clock chime eight times. It was about 200 yards to the print shop; I'd be late, *again*. Percy Dunlap, the print shop foreman, was sitting in the staff room smoking his foul-smelling briar pipe and reading the *Daily Herald* as I entered to hang up my raincoat and collect my dustcoat.

'You're late, Cholmondeley,' he said, looking at his silver pocket watch, the firm's award for 40 years' service. 'It's two minutes past eight. Everyone else is here and working. Why are you late?'

'I'm sorry,' I said, trying to sound contrite. 'It's the trams; you can't rely on them to be on time. They keep stopping and starting. The one I caught should have arrived at Southwark Bridge at 7.50, but it didn't get there until eight o'clock.'

'Then I suggest you catch an *earlier* tram. If you want to keep your job, get here on time,' Dunlap almost shouted.

I didn't reply. There was no point; he always got the last word in. I chose to ignore him while I searched for my dustcoat, which was hidden by my workmates' topcoats.

As I was about to leave the room, Dunlap called out to me: 'I've a job for you today. All our delivery vans are out all day, so I want you to hand deliver some urgently required contract forms to one of our best customers. The name of the firm is Keith Carlton-Smythe and his offices are in 4 Lloyds Avenue. The nearest tube station is Fenchurch Street. You can go straight after your lunch break. The forms will be available for collection from the dispatch bay. There are about thirty packs of 100 forms each, which amount to six reams of paper. That shouldn't be too much for a big lad like you to carry,' he said with a laugh.

'Consider it done, Mr Dunlap,' I said with enthusiasm, grateful for the chance of getting away from the print shop for a couple of hours. 'What about the train fare?' I added.

'Here's a shilling and that's more than enough to get you there and back. Don't forget my change when you return. Oh, yes, and save your tickets, as I'll need them to claim a refund from the cashier.'

I quickly devoured my lunch of spam sandwiches, thinking how much the Americans had done for our war effort by providing vast quantities of spam and dried eggs. With corned beef as part of the meat ration, usually saved to provide something to make a meat and vegetable pie in the middle of an almost meatless week, and a cheese ration of just about enough to bait a mousetrap, what would mothers have used to make sandwiches without them? I carefully washed my hands and face in cold water, with a sliver of Lifebuoy soap, combed my hair and carefully polished my shoes with Dunlap's discarded *Daily Herald*. I had seen pictures about city toffs and, although I was only delivering forms, I didn't want to look scruffy.

Collecting the forms from the dispatch bay I set off on my first unaccompanied journey on the underground railway. Arriving at Fenchurch Street Station, I found my way to Lloyds Avenue without difficulty. As I passed Lloyds of London, the internationally famous shipping insurance company, I recalled that when I was about eight years old my mother had taken me to see a film called *Lloyds of London*. It told the story of a young messenger boy who grew up to found the great insurance company. Who knows, I thought, the same thing might happen to me, but I'd rather have found something a bit more exciting than an insurance company. Something like a national newspaper or an international detective agency would be more up my street.

On entering 4 Lloyds Avenue, I saw a lift with its metal folding door open and a youngish, but weary looking, man standing at the opening and clutching a rope in his right hand. The office I wanted was on the second floor and normally I would have ignored a lift and raced up the stairs two or three at a time, but the large package of forms seemed to be getting heavier and more awkward to carry with every step I took.

'Second floor, please,' I said, as I entered the lift.

The liftman gave a deep sigh and shook his head, probably wondering why a fit looking youth would want to use a lift to the second floor.

'This parcel is very heavy and I've been carrying it a long way,' I offered lamely.

The liftman grinned, slammed the metal gate shut and pulled on the rope until the lift ascended and stopped at the second floor.

'Thanks mate,' I said, as I left the lift.

The liftman acknowledged my thanks with a smile, slammed the gate shut, as if he enjoyed the noise it made, and starting pushing the rope upwards through his prematurely gnarled hands.

I searched the long corridors until I found the office marked 'Keith Carlton-Smythe', obviously the boss's office. Next to it was a door marked 'General Office', which was the one I wanted. Holding the package of forms against my chest with one hand, I tapped lightly on the door.

'Come in,' a male voice called from within.

I opened the door and entered the office. 'Delivery of forms from Burlington's Printers, sir,' I announced, as if I bore *The Ten Commandants* on tablets of stone.

'Splendid, I was hoping they'd arrive today; they're urgently required. I'm most grateful for their speedy delivery. They look quite a load. Here, put them down on this desk. Have you carried them all the way from the printers?' asked the kindly faced, prematurely greying and bespectacled man, with a note of concern in his voice.

'I certainly have, sir,' I said, as I placed the package on the corner of his desk.

The man smiled warmly, displaying a set of tobacco and tea stained false teeth. 'My name is Humbledick, Charles Humbledick. I'm the office manager. There's no need to call me *sir*—Mr Humbledick will do fine.'

'OK, sir, I mean, Mr Humbledick. There's a receipt inside the top of the package. Our foreman said that the forms ought to be checked by the consignee before I left. Would you please look at them and if they are all right, sign the receipt and I'll be on my way.'

'Yes, of course I will. While I check them sit down and have a rest before you return', said Mr Humbledick, as he indicated a chair in the corner of the office.

While Mr Humbledick busied himself checking the forms, I spent my time looking around the office. I noted the old-fashioned and well-worn, but highly polished, office furniture, the oak framed pictures of ocean going ships and a large map of the world fixed to a notice board on the wall. The map had several dozen map pins stuck into it. From their positions on the map I judged them to indicate major seaports in foreign countries and was able to identify most of them. The study of maps had always been of interest to me.

Mr Humbledick completed his check of the forms and turned to me with a smile. 'These are perfect. I can't find a single error. Please tell Mr Burlington that Major Carlton-Smythe will be delighted with his work.'

'I certainly will,' I replied, as I stood up to leave.

'Hold on, son. Just a minute, I want to talk to you about something else. By the way, what is your name?'

'Archibald Cholmondeley, which is pronounced 'Chumly,' I replied, as I sat down, 'but I prefer to be called Archie.'

Mr Humbledick smiled. Amused, I guessed, by my unusual name— a cross I had learned to bear but was determined, when I became of age, to change it to a name that did not cause amusement or puzzlement.

'Well, Archie, I can quite understand you wishing to be called Archie. I'm sure many people have difficulty in pronouncing your surname.'

I nodded agreement.

'Tell me something about yourself. Are you happy in your present job?'

'No, not really, I find it very boring. It's not a bit like I expected it would be when I started.'

'Have you had any other jobs since you left school?'

'Yes, I've had rather a lot of different jobs, but none that I'd want to stay with.'

'How did you do at school?

'Oh, quite well, but I didn't get a chance to take a scholarship examination to get into a grammar school. Anyway, I had to leave school as soon as I could to get work to help my widowed mother.'

I was beginning to tire of Mr Humbledick's questions. He seemed genuine enough, but why should he be asking me all these questions? I was only delivering forms and I didn't feel inclined to unfold my life to a total stranger. Humbledick must have read my thoughts and he smiled encouragingly. 'Please go on, Archie; you seem to have had quite an eventful life for someone so young. Tell me, how's your knowledge of world geography?'

'It was one of my favourite subjects at school and I always wanted to get a job where I could use my knowledge of the world,' I replied enthusiastically, now warming to Mr Humbledick, and added, 'Something like a foreign correspondent.'

Humbledick looked at me steadily for a few seconds, then, leaning forward in his chair, said, in a confidential tone: 'We are currently looking for a youth to work here as my assistant. The last chap we had didn't stay long; he was called up and is likely to be in the army for some time. You seem like a bright young man. How would you like to work here?'

I swallowed hard. I couldn't believe what he was saying. Could this really be my chance to escape the tedious boredom of the print shop? 'Yes, sir, I certainly would, but I'd have to give at least one week's notice to my firm and then I'd have to work out how I could travel here. It takes me over an hour by tram to get from Woolwich to Southwark Bridge, which means that I have to leave my home at about six thirty to catch a tram from Woolwich.'

'No problems there,' he replied with a laugh. 'I'll ring your boss about your notice. We're very good customers of his, so I'm sure he'll not object to our request. As to getting here, I'm sure you'll have a better journey by Southern Railway than by those clanking old trams to Southwark Bridge. We don't open the office until nine so you've plenty of time to walk from London Bridge or Cannon Street Station. We close the office at four thirty, so you would be getting home much earlier than you do in your present job.'

'Yes, I certainly would. At present it's nearly seven before I get home.'

This was getting better by the moment. Before I could think of a suitable answer Mr Humbledick continued, 'Wait here, Archie, I'll ring your boss from the major's office. The major isn't here today. He lives in Wiltshire and only comes in about once a week to sign contracts and letters, and see our contracted shipowners.'

Mr Humbledick went into the major's office and shortly afterwards I could hear him having a conversation with someone on the telephone. I strained my ears, but could not hear what he was saying. I thought it unwise to listen at the door, as there was always the chance that Humbledick would suddenly come out of the office and catch me eavesdropping. Too much was at stake to do that.

Humbledick returned after a few minutes. 'Good news, Archie, I've spoken to Mr Burlington and he is quite agreeable to you giving just two days' notice and leaving this Friday, which means you can start here on Monday. Is that all right with you?'

'Yes, sir, I mean Mr Humbledick, that's fine. I'll be here sharp at nine on Monday,' I said, and meant it.

His decision to give me the job had put me in a state of euphoria. I would be working fewer hours a week and yet be paid ten shillings a week more. Riches indeed, I thought, as I calculated its worth in cinema tickets and cigarettes.

*   *   *   *

'I must say you look pleased with yourself tonight, Archie,' said my mother, as she placed a portion of her meat and vegetable pie on my plate. 'Have you been given a rise or something?'

'Well, sort of. I've got a new job, in an office, a ship chandlers' agent's firm. The owner is a retired army officer called Major Keith Carlton-Smythe. I start on Monday.'

My mother sat down and looked at me enquiringly; she wanted to hear more. She was used to me moving from job to job, but always hoped that I might find a really worthwhile one and make a career of it. She had told me many times that she regretted that, because of our constant moving about the country, I had been unable to sit my scholarship examination and go on for further education. She had hoped that an apprenticeship in the printing trade might be the answer.

'However did you manage to find a job like that?'

'I don't really know. Mr Humbledick, he's the manager of the firm, didn't seem to be bothered by my lack of educational qualifications. He seemed more interested in my knowledge of world geography and the fact that I had worked in such a variety of occupations at such an early age. Mind you, I expect he was probably anxious to replace his last assistant, who had been called up for the army. So I expect I came along at the right time and saved them the trouble of advertising and interviewing a lot of school-leavers.'

My mother beamed and grasped my hand across the table. 'Oh, Archie, I'm so pleased you've got a proper job that you might settle into. Of course, working in a city office, you'll have to look smart, especially since you'll be working for a retired army officer. You'll have to be on your best behaviour at all times and you'll need to wear a suit and a collar and tie. We must get all your best clothes ready this weekend, but eat your dinner now, before it gets cold. I've got some bread pudding for afters and I know how much you like my bread puddings.'

I smiled, nodded my agreement and then continued my search among the mixture of vegetables for traces of the couple of slices of corned beef that made up the meat ingredient of my mother's meat and vegetable pie.

CHAPTER 2

▼

It was Sunday, the day before I was to start my new job. I had prepared all my clothes and checked on the times of the workmen's trains to London Bridge and Cannon Street. The latest workmen's train would get me to London about an hour before I needed to be there, but the fares were much cheaper.

I usually went to the cinema with my close friend, Cyril Magwick, on Sunday afternoons. They always showed old films on Sundays. They were usually 'A' films, which meant that you had to be accompanied by an adult, or be over 16 to be admitted to the cinema. This was no problem for me, for when I put on my long raincoat and wore a trilby, I looked about 18 and nobody ever asked to see my identity card. If Cyril, who looked no older than his age, were refused admittance, as soon as the lights went out and the programme started, I would walk down the aisle to the toilets and let him in through the adjacent fire escape door. Unfortunately, our Sunday visit to the cinema would have to wait until next week when I received my first wage packet from Keith Carlton-Smythe. In the meantime I needed what little cash I had to pay my train fares.

With little else to do but read, I spent Sunday afternoon giving thought to what opportunities there might be for me to make a little money out of my new job. Not much hope there, though. Mr Humbledick had told me that the only 'resources', for which I would be responsible, would be a postage stamp register. All letters had to be booked out in the register and against every entry the value of the stamp used had to be shown.

I thought of the previous money making schemes I had employed since we had moved back to London. Apart from running errands for elderly neighbours at a penny an errand, my first successful scheme had been selling bundles of firewood. Cyril and I would collect old floorboards and any other pieces of timber that we found lying amid the ruins of bombed houses. We would carry the timber to my backyard, where we would chop it up into small sticks, suitably sized for lighting fires. We bundled up about 15 sticks and tied them up with string. These were delivered to our customers for a penny a bundle. We undercut the local hardware store, or 'Oil Shop' as everyone called it, because the shop's biggest sale was paraffin for oil stoves, and they charged a penny ha'penny for about ten sticks of firewood.

This business had kept Cyril and me in cinema and cigarette money for several months, but suitable wood became harder to find as local bombed sites were rapidly being cleared of debris. What finally put the kibosh on our wood collecting operations occurred one Sunday morning when we were out scavenging for wood.

At the back of the Lord Herbert public house in Herbert Road, Plumstead, was a large bomb-damaged brick outbuilding. It had probably been some sort of stable for horses 50 or more years previously. Its roof was heavily timbered and supported, what must have been at one time, an attractive roof garden. All that now remained on top was an eight-inch deep zinc container, filled with moss-covered soil.

Cyril and I explored the interior, noting the beams that could be sawn into lengths and were suitable for chopping up for firewood.

'How are we going to get those beams down?' asked Cyril. 'The ceiling is at least ten feet high.'

'Shouldn't be too much of a problem,' I said, with more confidence than I felt. 'Those beams are only resting on the edges of the brick walls; if we give the walls a bang with one of these stout timbers, the beams should be dislodged.'

Cyril didn't share my confidence in what I proposed. 'Sounds a bit dodgy to me. I think I'll stand outside and watch.'

'Yes, do that. There's no point in both of us being at risk.'

I picked up a six-foot length of four by two timber and repeatedly jabbed it hard against the back wall of the building. The brick wall shuddered and some of the beams slipped to the edge of their supporting bricks. 'It's coming!' I cried excitedly.

Suddenly, there was a loud cracking noise above my head. The sudden realisation of what I had done made me aware that I was now in imminent danger. There was a hole in the base of the wall, no more than two or three foot square. My instinct for survival caused me to move faster than I had ever done before. I dived through the hole as though I had been fired from a cannon and most of me was out by the time the whole roof fell in. Luckily for me, the only thing that hit me was a pile of wet soil.

A white-faced Cyril rushed over to me. 'You crazy bleeder, Archie, you're lucky you weren't killed.'

I forced a laugh, stood up and shook the soil from my trousers and shoes.

'Now I know what they mean when they say that someone has "brought the house down".'

The noise brought the Sunday lunchtime drinkers rushing out of the pub.

'I'm sure that a bomb has dropped at the back of the pub,' one shouted.

'But I didn't hear an air raid siren,' shouted another.

It was time for a hurried departure from the scene and we didn't stop running until we reached the foot of the stone steps leading up to Cyril's house.

We had paper rounds, of course. These earned us a few shillings a week, but it meant getting up at about five o'clock in the morning and delivering about 100 newspapers, magazines and comics in the black-out. With just a very small torch, we used to read the number scrawled on the top of the paper, but the dim light it afforded had to be carefully shielded, or you stood every chance of having, 'Put that light out!' shouted at you by an ARP (Air Raid Precautions) Warden.

✳   ✳   ✳   ✳

I had left school in April 1944 and was working at my first job as an assistant in a pawnbroker and jeweller's shop, when the Allied Forces landed in France. Immediately after D-Day the Germans started sending their flying bombs or 'doodlebugs', as we called them, against London.

My mother was travelling by rail from Woolwich when two flying bombs crashed alongside the train. She was injured and suffered extreme shock. After treatment in the local hospital she was advised by her doctor to leave London and stay in the country until she had recovered from her experience. A family friend, who had relatives in High Wycombe, arranged for my mother and me to stay with them.

I needed a job, so as soon as we had got settled into our temporary home I went to the local labour exchange.

'You're rather young for any of the vacancies we have,' said the snooty-faced clerk as he consulted his register of job vacancies. 'Ah, here's one, it's for a recent school leaver to train as an apprentice plumber. Are you interested in that?'

'No, and I'm not likely to be here for long, just a few months at most.'

'Oh, then it's *temporary* work you are seeking? That's even more difficult for someone of your age. Employers usually want their temporary employees to have had experience of the work, or to have received appropriate training. You hardly fill the bill, do you?'

I was beginning to dislike this pompous twerp. He was supposed to help me find a job. 'Look, pal, I badly need work. I have a widowed mother to help support. I'll do anything within reason. You must have *something* to offer.'

The clerk turned the pages of his register again. 'Hmm, here's a vacancy that has only just arisen. It's working as a porter in the American Red Cross Aero Club at their base near Wycombe Abbey. It's only a few minutes walk from here. They don't specify how old applicants should be, but it's most unlikely that they would take on anyone as young as you.'

'I'm big for my age and quite strong,' I retorted. 'I really do need a job and I could lie about my age, say that I was seventeen. Please let me try anyway.' I was almost pleading now.

'Yes, I suppose you are quite big for your age and strong enough, I imagine, but you won't be able lie about your age, because I shall have to put it on your introductory card.'

'So you're going to let me apply for the job, then?'

'Yes, but I shouldn't hold out too much hope of getting it,' said Snooty-Face, as he completed the introductory card.

'When you get to the base you must report to the guardroom just inside the gate and show this card to whoever is in charge. They'll then arrange to have you taken to the American Red Cross HQ. The ARC does all the hiring of civilian staff for the Aero Club.'

When I arrived at the base a soldier carrying a rifle on his shoulder stopped me at the gate. I showed him my introductory card, which he ignored.

'Report to the sergeant of the guard over there,' he said, pointing to a grim looking brick building.

I entered the guardroom and handed my card to the leathery faced, multi-striped NCO, with a large area of his left breast covered with an adornment of campaign medal ribbons. I was reminded of the fruit salads my mother made before wartime rationing came in. The NCO read the card and returned it to me.

'Archibald Sinclair Cholmondeley, is that your real name?' he asked, disbelievingly.

'Yes, sir, that is my name; my surname is pronounced Chumly, but I prefer to be called Archie. You must have heard of *that* name before. It's the British film star Cary Grant's real name—Archibald, Archibald Leach.'

'Sure, kid, I've heard of that Limey actor, he's one of my old lady's favourites. Sit over there,' he said, pointing at a chair near the door, 'and I'll rustle up a driver to take you up the hill to the Aero Club.'

The NCO stood up, opened the door at the back of the office and shouted, 'Kowalski, get your butt in here, I've got a job for you!'

A few seconds later a young, overweight soldier, with a single inverted chevron on his sleeve, rushed into the office and stood in front of the NCO. The NCO winked at the soldier, who came smartly to attention. 'PFC Kowalski, reporting and awaiting your instructions, first sergeant.'

The sergeant gave a sly grin. 'Kowalski, I want you to drive this young gentleman up to Colonel Pollock's Red Cross offices. He's to be interviewed for a job at the Aero Club, but he'll need to be seen by Miss Eicher first.'

'Consider it done, first sergeant,' then to me he said, 'let's go, sir.'

I was beginning to get the feeling that they were both play-acting to take the rise out of me, but I didn't give a fig as I wanted the job too much to bother about anyone making a joke at my expense. I accompanied Kowalski outside, where he climbed into a jeep that was parked a few yards away from the guardroom.

'Climb aboard, kid.'

I eagerly complied; I was looking forward to my first journey in a jeep. Two or three minutes of driving up the winding, tree lined road to the top of the hill and Kowalski stopped the jeep outside a large, single storey, corrugated iron roofed building. A sign above the main entrance read, 'AERO CLUB'.

'This is it, kid—the Aero Club. Report to Helen Eicher's office, second on the left down the corridor. Oh, yeah, and if you get the job, don't expect to be driven up the hill every morning as transportation is only given to officers and senior non-coms. Junior enlisted men and civilian employees are expected to use Shanks's pony,' Kowalski shouted above the noise of the jeep's engine, as he revved the motor.

'Thanks, Yank, I'll remember that,' I shouted back.

I tapped on the door marked 'Helen Eicher'.

'Come in,' a distinctly American female voice invited.

I opened the door, strode briskly into the office and stopped in front of Miss Eicher's desk. She looked up at me enquiringly and smiled.

'I'm Archie Cholmondeley, pronounced Chumly' I said, as I placed my introductory card on the desk in front of her. 'I've been sent from the labour exchange for an interview for the job you advertised.'

Miss Eicher, an attractive brunette, I guessed to be in her mid-thirties, picked up the card and looked at it briefly. She then looked me up and down in a way that made me flush with embarrassment.

'My, my, you *are* a big lad. I can't believe you're only 14. Shouldn't you still be at school?'

Before I could think of an answer, she invited me to sit down, indicating a chair in the corner of the office. I sat in the chair, crossed my arms in front of my chest and put on a serious and, what I thought to be, an eager and alert expression. 'I'm 15 in January,' I blurted out, defensively. 'I left school in April and started work straight away. My mother is a widow, so I need to work to help out.'

Miss Eicher gave me a sympathetic look, then smiled. 'Well, I must say you look fit and strong enough to do the job we have on offer. If we decide to offer you the job and you accept it, you would be under the supervision of the club caretaker, Mr Bagshot, who is responsible to the club manager, Master Sergeant Hiram Guggenheimer. Your primary duties would be to light all the coke stoves in the club every morning and keep them stoked up until you cease work at five o'clock. You would also be responsible for keeping the club library tidy and replacing the books in alphabetical order of authors on the shelves. Another of your more important responsibilities would be the unloading of the vehicles bringing the weekly delivery of Coca-Cola and Pepsi Cola to the base, stacking the crates in the club store, and loading the crates of empty bottles onto the delivery lorries. Do you think you could manage to carry out those duties without any difficulty?'

I straightened myself up in the chair and put on a purposeful expression. 'Yes, ma'am, I feel sure I could. I'm very strong for my age. I can carry a sack of King Edward's potatoes at least two miles and lift a hundredweight bag of cement. As for books, I love them. I used to read one every day. And lighting fires is right up my street. I often used to light the fire at home and I was once the patrol cook when I went camping with the Boy Scouts, and had to light fires every day with bits of dead tree wood.'

Miss Eicher gave a soft laugh. 'You won't have much time for reading here, but I think you'll do for us, Archie. I'll have a quick word with Colonel Pollock. He's no longer in the army, but he is the top American Red Cross man on the base. If he agrees, you can start on Monday. As to your salary, we wouldn't be able to make it any more than two pounds ten shillings a week; that's more than ten dollars. Would that be acceptable to you?'

Fifty shillings a week! I couldn't believe it. I knew the Yanks were well paid, but that was twice as much as I had been getting at the pawnshop. 'Yes, ma'am, that sounds reasonable enough,' I croaked.

Retired Colonel Pollock agreed that I could be employed and Miss Eicher introduced me to the club manager, a friendly-faced giant of a man in his mid-thirties, and the caretaker, a thin, wispy-haired and craggy faced man of about fifty.

'Are you any good at lighting fires? The ones here are pot stoves and we have to light them with wood and coke. They're real sods to get going. You really need a bit of coal to get the coke started, but that's very scarce and the little they do get is used in the officers' club,' said Bagshot.

'Yes, lots, Mr Bagshot, I often lit the fire at home and I was a patrol cook with the Boy Scouts and had to light fires with whatever I could find that would burn.'

'What did you do, rub two of the Boy Scouts together to get the fire started?'

Thinking it wise to humour Bagshot—after all, he was my boss—I joined in his guffawing at the tired old joke that must have been in circulation since 1908 when the Boy Scout Movement was formed. This seemed to please him and he was all smiles as he showed me around the club, finishing up in the kitchen, where he persuaded the duty cook to make two mugs of coffee and produce a plate of chocolate 'cookies', as he called them.

I watched in astonishment as he shovelled three or four heaped spoonfuls of brown sugar into his mug. No shortage of food here, I thought, as I followed suit.

We drank our coffee and ate our cookies in silence. Bagshot seemed in a hurry to get back to work and I could not think of anything worthwhile to say that was more important than enjoying the rare treat of eating chocolate biscuits and sampling real coffee, after having only ever drunk nothing better than Camp coffee. Anyway, I had always been told not to talk with my mouth full.

When Bagshot moved away from the table to talk to one of the civilian kitchen hands, I quickly grabbed three or four of the biscuits and put them into my jacket pocket—they were too good to pass up. Bagshot returned to the table, glanced at the empty plate and smiled. 'I'll see you here on Monday morning then, eight o'clock sharp. The mornings are always very busy, what with the fires to get lit and clearing up the mess they make in the club overnight,' he said as he escorted me out of the club.

'I'll be here with bells on, Mr Bagshot, you can depend upon it,' I replied as I set out on my long walk back to the main gate.

Bagshot wasn't kidding when he said the stoves were hard to light, I thought, as I coaxed the coke to burn with slivers of wood and screwed up sheets of *The Stars and Stripes*, the US servicemen's newspaper; better known by the troops as 'The Stares and Strips'. It took me the best part of the morning to get all the stoves going, but after a few days I finally mastered the task and was encouraged by the praise heaped on me by the near frozen GIs who came in from the late autumn cold to warm themselves and take their refreshment breaks in the club.

'We could sure do with a guy like you to keep us warm in our hut at night,' shrilled one blowsy looking WAC, as she waggled her tight trousered fanny (a new American word to me) in front of the stove.

I pretended that I thought she referred to keeping their hut stove going throughout the night, and continued pouring more coke into the glowing red stove.

Working in the library was a rewarding experience for a book lover like me. Every author I had ever heard of, and hundreds I hadn't, were represented. After stoking up all the stoves, I would settle myself in an armchair in the far corner of the library, which was usually empty for most of the day apart from break times, and select a paperback book from the well-filled book shelves that covered most of the wall space in the room. I was introduced to the classics—books like Pearl Buck's *Good Earth*, John Steinbeck's *The Grapes of Wrath*, James Hilton's *Lost Horizon* and Margaret Mitchell's *Gone with the Wind*, but it was detective fiction I usually chose to read. I found books featuring detectives I had only before seen on the cinema screen; sleuths like Sherlock Holmes, Ellery Queen, Hugh 'Bulldog' Drummond, Lord Peter Wimsey, Nero Wolfe, Sam Spade, Hercule Poirot, Michael Shayne and Philip Marlowe.

During one such stolen absence from my duties, slumped in a sumptuous armchair and deeply immersed in one of Hercule Poirot's cases, I felt my cigarette lighter slip from the pocket of my overalls. As I reached to retrieve it, down it went, between the well-depressed seat and the arm of the chair. I pushed my hand down after it, and as I withdrew it from under the seat, it came into contact with a miscellany of other items. I gathered them up and found numerous coins from pennies to half-crowns, as well as penknives, combs, cigarette lighters, packets of chewing gum and, most surprising of all, packets of French letters. I quickly gathered up the coins and put them into my pocket. Nobody would miss those and, in any case, who was to say to whom they belonged? The losers could probably identify the lighters, pen-knives and other items, so those I took to the manager's office.

'Now that's what I call honesty, kid, honesty that deserves to be rewarded. The guys who lost these items will sure be pleased to get them back. Do you like chocolate bars and gum, kid?' asked Master Sergeant Guggenheimer with a broad grin.

'Yes, sir, I certainly do, and I haven't had many of those since the war started,' I replied.

'Well, here, you take these, kid,' said the sergeant as he handed me a dozen or more O'Henry bars and a box of packets of chewing gum he had taken from a cupboard in the corner of his office.

I was on easy street. What with my two pounds ten shillings weekly wage, two pounds of which I gave to my mother, my continued plun-dering of the cash laden armchairs and the club manager's rewards for my honesty in returning the various items I found, I was able to indulge myself and the son of the landlady with whom we lodged, with treats to the cinema, cigarettes and sweets. I also attracted a large fol-lowing of the neighbourhood's youngsters, who would call out to me, like they did to American servicemen: 'Got any gum chum?' I'd get a great kick out of tossing them a packet or two and watch them scram-ble for possession.

My new source of income nearly came to a sudden halt when Bag-shot made a surprise visit to the library, something he rarely did, prob-ably just to borrow a book, or have a crafty nap in an out-of-view armchair. As cash and other valuables were becoming difficult to access down the sides of the armchairs, I had decided to tip them all upside down and shake the coins and other items down so that they could be reached from under the seats.

'What the blue blazes are you doing with those chairs?' bawled Bagshot, more in panic than anger.

'Oh, just cleaning them,' I said with a nonchalance I didn't feel. 'They are all very dusty underneath, thick with dust and cobwebs. I think there must be spiders hibernating in the chairs so I'm giving them a good spring clean.'

Bagshot gaped in awe. 'We've never done that before. You could have damaged the chairs or injured yourself, turning them over like that on your own. I'll get one of the other porters to come in and give you a hand to put them back on their feet.'

'Don't bother, Mr Bagshot, I'm very strong for my age and can manage these on my own,' I replied, fearful that someone else might stumble on my treasure trove if they handled the chairs.

Bagshot grunted, shrugged his shoulders and left the library.

*   *   *   *

Hitler's last major offensive, the Battle of the Bulge, had been thwarted and the war was coming to a close, although V2 rockets were still falling on London and the Home Counties.

My mother's decision to return to London coincided with a run down of both military and civilian personnel at the base.

Master Sergeant Guggenheimer called me to his office. 'This reconnaissance wing has ceased operations and we are shipping men back stateside,' he explained. 'The Aero Club is to close down and the ARC group are going home. This means that you and the other domestic staff will no longer be required. You're to get a month's severance pay and a letter of thanks, personally signed by General Doolittle, for your services.'

'That's OK with me, sergeant, as my mother wants to get back home to London anyway. She's heard that the house has been damaged by a V2 rocket and will need a lot of repairs doing to it.'

'That's too bad, kid. I'm real sorry to hear that. Those Nazi sons of bitches are really giving you British folks a hell of a hard time in London. Never mind, it should be all over soon.'

'I certainly hope so, sergeant. By the way, if the Aero Club is closing down, what will you be doing with all the paperback books in the library?' I asked, a new idea for making money entering my mind.

'I guess those that are not taken by the guys when they leave will be sent for paper salvage. Why, do *you* want some of them? If you do then help yourself to as many as you want.'

'I'd really appreciate that. Thanks a million, sergeant.'

'You're welcome, kid, you've done a great job in keeping this club warm and you've kept the library neat. You've also made a lot of guys happy by finding and returning their lost property. When you leave I have a large case of O'Henry bars to give you as a farewell gift.'

'Thanks, sergeant, they'll be welcome when I get back to London and sweet rationing again.'

My mother's shout up the stairs, 'Come on down, Archie, your dinner's on the table and getting cold,' brought me back from thoughts of my days at the American base.

CHAPTER 3

▼

Starting work on the Monday morning, I arrived at about eight o'clock, having caught a workmen's train (the cost was half the normal fare, provided you caught the train before seven o'clock) to Cannon Street Station and walking to Lloyds Avenue.

As previously instructed by the office manager, I collected the general office key from the building superintendent's office, let myself in and explored both offices, entering the major's office through the interconnecting door in the general office. In the middle of the general office, where there had been a large area of floor space when Charles Humbledick had interviewed me for the job, there now stood an antique looking desk. I thought its ornate moulded legs, edges and odd-shaped pulling handles would have looked more at home in a Victoriana museum rather than a modern business office. On it was a very ancient looking Remington typewriter, a desk blotter, two well-worn wicker trays labelled 'in' and 'out', a pen and pencil rack, and two silver-capped inkwells.

Not bad, not bad at all, I thought, I think I'm going to like it here. With nothing to do but await the arrival of Mr Humbledick, who wouldn't be in the office for at least another 45 minutes, I put my feet up on the desk, lit my first Player's Weight of the day and began to ponder over what my duties would entail and what opportunities there might be to enable me to supplement my income.

*   *   *   *

It was Wednesday, the day that the boss, Major (mustn't forget his military rank) Carlton-Smythe, came to the office. It was to be my first meeting with him since I had started with the firm and I was anxious to create a good impression. I was wearing my best suit, actually my only suit that an uncle had given me when he joined the army. 'It won't fit me when I come out, so you might as well get some use out of it,' he had said. I had pressed the trousers, changed my shirt collar and taken great pains over polishing my shoes the night before.

Mr Humbledick had arrived at the office at about nine fifteen on Monday and Tuesday, but today he was in at 8.55 a.m. It occurred to me that he did not want to risk arriving late, in case the major arrived earlier than expected.

'Have you collected the cablegrams this morning?' he asked, as he placed his raincoat, trilby and umbrella on the hatstand.

'Yes, sir, I mean, Mr Humbledick, I went to Cable and Wireless and Commercial Cable on my way from the station,' I said, handing him about a dozen cablegrams.

He took them to his desk under the window, and quickly scanned their contents, muttering, almost soundlessly. 'Hmm, prices are on the up again. Well, you know what to do with them, don't you?' he said, as he reached over to my desk and dropped them into my in-tray.

The cablegrams were all from ship chandlers, or 'our principals', as Mr Humbledick called them, whom we represented in the United Kingdom. They advised changes in the prices of food and other commodities—everything from apples to yeast—and supplied merchant ships owned by the companies we had contracted on their behalf to purchase their supplies. We received five per cent of the payments made to the ship chandlers for the goods they supplied. My task was to amend ship chandlers' price lists. Not in manuscript, for Major Carlton-Smythe insisted that, for neatness sake, the amendments had to be typed as near as possible to the deleted price. The amendments were quite simple, just a matter of changing a price against an item. Since there were sometimes several hundred lists to amend, I used carbon paper and amended about six copies at a time. I was no touch-typist, but I had some experience of two-finger typing on a second-hand typewriter my mother had bought me when she had hopes that I might get a job with a newspaper. Mr Humbledick couldn't touch type either, but he had been two-finger typing for about 20 years and could rattle along at great speed when he was typing letters to our principals and contracted shipowners.

'You'll be able to type as fast as me with two fingers when you've had a few years' practise,' he forecasted, with a laugh.

We were both typing. Mr Humbledick was composing a cablegram to a ship chandler in Montevideo on his relatively new war finish Imperial typewriter and I was amending the price of bananas in Las Palmas on my ancient Remington machine. Neither of us heard the office door open.

'Good morning, that's what I like to see, my staff hard at it,' boomed the voice of Major Carlton-Smythe from the doorway.

We both stopped typing and stood up at our desks; something I had been briefed to do by Mr Humbledick, whenever the major or his 'lady' entered the office. The major walked into the office, closely followed by Mrs Carlton-Smythe.

'Good morning, sir, good morning, Mrs Carlton-Smythe,' we said in chorus.

'I have all the week's correspondence and cash ledgers to hand if you want to go through them, sir,' Humbledick said in an obsequious tone that I had not heard from him before.

'Later, Humbledick, later', the major replied testily. 'I want to have a word or two with this young man you've recruited.'

Humbledick, looking nonplussed, sat at his desk and pored over the morning's post. I remained standing at my desk, under the close scrutiny of the major and Mrs Carlton-Smythe.

'You're a big lad for 15; how tall are you?'

'About six feet, sir,' I replied, raising myself to my full height, to become as tall as the immaculately grey-suited, florid-faced, black haired and bristle moustached man who confronted me.

'Ever thought about a career in the military, lad?'

'Yes, sir, I tried to get into the Royal Marine Commandos—under age. I passed the medical, but they found out my true age and offered me a cadetship in the Marine Band. But as the only musical instrument I've ever played is the comb and tissue paper, I didn't accept their offer.'

The major sighed deeply. He obviously didn't think much of my little joke.

'Yes, he is a smart looking lad and I think he'd look good in uniform, Keith,' interposed Mrs Carlton-Smythe, who had been looking me over while the major was talking to me.

'Yes, Claudia, he is. I had a lot like him, at his age, serving and dying under my command in the Great War, but now I'm more concerned about his abilities as a clerk rather than his potential as an infantryman.'

Mrs Carlton-Smythe looked hurt and changed the subject.

'Oh look, Keith, the drawers of Cholmondeley's desk have pear drop handles. How delightful—I haven't seen handles like that for years. Where did you get this desk?'

'Oh, I don't know. Humbledick found it in some second-hand furniture shop. It only cost a couple of guineas, but it does the job,' the major replied irritably. 'Anyway, Claudia, I haven't got time to waste talking about the office furniture. I thought you wanted to do some shopping and have some lunch with friends up west. I've got plenty of business to talk over with Humbledick before I leave so you get off to Oxford Street to do your shopping and meet your friends for lunch and I'll meet you at Paddington in time to get the three fifty train to Warminster.'

'But, Keith dear, I shan't be able to do much shopping; I've no clothing coupons left.'

'Well, Claudia, I can't do anything about that; you've used all mine as well. You shouldn't be so extravagant; you've far too many clothes anyway. I make my clothes last for years. I haven't had a new suit since before the war.'

While they were talking, I had taken the opportunity to sit down at my desk and record the morning's post in the office mail book, but I was listening carefully to the Carlton-Smythes' conversation regarding clothing coupons, and an idea had occurred to me that might provide an opportunity to make some cash. I waited for the right moment, when the major, followed by Humbledick clutching a sheaf of papers and the cash journal, went into his office. Mrs Carlton-Smythe was about to leave the office.

'Please allow me,' I said, as I quickly crossed the office and opened the door, with an exaggerated flourish.

'Thank you, Cholmondeley,' Mrs Carlton-Smythe said with a smile. 'I'm glad to see that the age of chivalry has not been lost with your generation.'

'No…er…madam,' I stammered, anxious not to lose the opportunity to put my idea into practice. 'I hope you won't think me forward, but I couldn't help hearing your conversation with your husband. You said that you had used up all your clothing coupons.'

'Yes, I'm afraid so, they don't go far when you have to keep up appearances at all the functions that the major and I have to attend.'

'Well, madam, I think I might be able to help you.'

'Really, please tell me how. I'm interested.'

'I might be able to get some for you. Of course they'd cost you at least a couple of bob each,' I said, trying not to sound like a black marketeer.

'Oh, you *wonderful* boy, that would be such a help to me if you could. How soon can you get them? I'm coming into town with the major next Wednesday, and if you have them for me then, I'd be willing to pay you as much as half a crown for a coupon.'

'I'll do my very best to get them for you by next Wednesday,' I said in a low voice.

'Thank you so much, Archie. It is Archie, isn't it?' she whispered, as she grasped my left hand and gave it a gentle squeeze.

'Yes, Mrs Carlton-Smythe, that's what everyone calls me,' I said, giving her a broad grin.

'Goodbye, see you next Wednesday,' she said, as she walked down the corridor.

I closed the door quietly, went back to my desk and lit a cigarette. That had been easy, perhaps *too* easy. Mrs Carlton-Smythe was a real pushover, but the major was something else; I'd have to watch my step with him. I'd been told he was 63, but by the way he looked and moved about, he could have passed for fifty. I guessed Mrs Carlton-Smythe to be in her early fifties. They'd probably got married when he came home from the war. Humbledick had confided that they didn't have any children, possibly because of the rather nasty wound the major had sustained in the fighting at Passchendaele, in the Great War. I guessed that the major and Humbledick would be some time in the office going over the week's work; time enough for me to relax for a while until lunchtime. I felt so good, I thought I'd celebrate by going to the ABC restaurant and treat myself to one of their special, but cheap, lunches: sausage and chips, college pudding with custard, roll and butter, and a cup of tea, one and a penny the lot.

The opening of the major's interconnecting door disturbed my thoughts. Mr Humbledick's head appeared around the door. 'Cholmondeley!' Humbledick shouted in a military drill instructor's voice, no doubt for the major's benefit, 'the major wants you to collect his order of sandwiches from the delicatessen in Fenchurch Street. Here's half a crown—look lively, lad!'

I snatched the proffered coin from Humbledick's hand and dashed from the office as if it were on fire. I could play the silly ass as well as anybody else.

CHAPTER 4

▼

It was late morning. Mr Humbledick and I were both busy sorting the mail and cablegrams for price changes when the major, accompanied by his wife, entered the office.

'Good morning,' was the brusque greeting from the major to us, and then he turned to his wife. 'I won't be more than 20 minutes with Humbledick, Claudia; why don't you wait for me here and we can then go off together to meet the Lamberts for luncheon at the Strand Palace Hotel', the major suggested, pointing at the visitors' chair in the corner of the office. 'I'm sure young Cholmondeley will be happy to keep you company. Why not send him down to the kiosk for a news-paper—the *Daily Telegraph*; I didn't have time to get one at the station this morning.'

'Yes, I'll be quite happy to wait for you, dear. You go ahead, and don't rush on my account,' replied Mrs Carlton-Smythe, as the major and Humbledick entered the major's office.

Mrs Carlton-Smythe turned to face me and smiled sweetly.

'Archie, I do hope you've been able to obtain some clothing cou-pons for me,' she said in a plaintive tone. 'There are one or two essen-tial items of underclothing I desperately need.'

I bet one of them is a corset, she certainly needs one, I thought unkindly.

'Well, madam, I was unable to get any coupons for less that four bob each from my usual sources, but not to worry, I can let you have ten of my own coupons for the price you agreed last week. I'm afraid that's the best I can do at the moment. Is that all right?'

'That's absolutely splendid, Archie. Now let's see, what did I promise? Half a crown wasn't it?' she said, as she took a purse out of her enormous, black leather handbag.

'That's right,' I said, as I withdrew a brown envelope from my inside jacket pocket and handed it to her.

Mrs Carlton-Smythe almost snatched the envelope from my hand and without opening it, stuffed it into her handbag. She opened her purse and withdrew a pound note, two half-crowns and a shilling from it.

'Here you are, Archie, here's your money and I've added a little bonus for you—you being so helpful.'

I took the money and quickly put it in my jacket pocket. 'Thank you, madam; do you want me to keep you in mind if I have any more for sale?'

'Yes, I certainly do. As many as you can get, but you'll have to save them for me, because I only come into town about once a month.'

'OK, madam, I'll be happy to do—'

I stopped short as the door opened and the major, followed by Humbledick clutching his cash journal, strode quickly over to where Mrs Carlton-Smythe and I were standing.

'Here we are then, Claudia, I didn't keep you waiting too long did I?' boomed the major, as if he were shouting commands on a parade ground.

'No, dear, you didn't. As usual, your timing was impeccable, but you had no need to hurry because young Cholmondeley has been entertaining me with stories about his previous jobs. I feel sure that he has great potential and should go a long way in the world of commerce.'

'Splendid, did you hear that, Humbledick? You picked a winner for a change. Mrs Carlton-Smythe is a very shrewd judge of character and is rarely wrong about such things.'

'Can we go now, Keith, I'm beginning to feel famished,' said Mrs Carlton-Smythe.

The major gave a deep sigh. 'Yes, Claudia, we can go now, but I did tell you that you should have had some breakfast before we left this morning.'

As Mrs Carlton-Smythe followed her husband out of the office, she turned and giving a little wave said: 'Goodbye Archie, goodbye Humbledick.'

'Goodbye, madam,' was Humbledick's response, but I just grinned and gave her a cheeky wink.

Mrs Carlton-Smythe and I had quickly established a relationship, which might be of benefit to both of us, I thought, as I touched the crisp pound note and coins in my jacket pocket.

A little later, as I sat at my desk eating my lunch of dried egg sandwiches, and Humbledick was ramming tobacco into his pipe bowl, he paused and turned to me. 'You seemed to have hit it off very well with Mrs Carlton-Smythe. She's never been very friendly to me, let alone the office boys; usually ignores them completely.'

'Oh, she probably recognises my natural charm,' I replied with a grin.

'More likely she wishes you were a few years older and willing to give her something she's not been getting very much of lately. You are rather a big boy for your age and Mrs Carlton-Smythe is said to prefer big men,' said Humbledick with an uncharacteristic leer.

I gave an embarrassed laugh and bit into one of my mother's aptly named rock cakes.

CHAPTER 5

▼

The war was over and the war criminals, well those on the losing side, were being tried for their crimes against humanity. Rationing was still on, but things were beginning to improve gradually, and the newly elected Labour Party promised us a rosier future.

I had a lucrative little business going on; buying clothing coupons from some of my old school friends for two shillings each and selling them to Mrs Carlton-Smythe for three and sixpence. This income kept me in cigarettes, the occasional lunch at the ABC restaurant and a couple of visits to the local cinemas each week, but my sources were fast beginning to dry up—well, at least for the current year and, anyway, surely clothes rationing couldn't last much longer? I had to think of another way of supplementing my meagre weekly wage. A solution came sooner than I expected.

Humbledick was busy balancing the petty cash and I was opening the mail for him to read. I date-stamped the letters and affixed them to the appropriate files. When this had been done I salvaged any envelopes that could be reused, by sticking economy labels on them, and placed them in the 'envelope box' for future use. The building caretaker would put other unusable envelopes in a special salvaged paper bin for collection.

Pausing to light his pipe, Humbledick turned to me and watched my progress. 'You're not throwing away envelopes with foreign stamps on them, are you?' Humbledick exclaimed in horror. 'The major would throw a fit if he saw you doing that. I did tell you when you first started here that all foreign stamps were to be carefully cut off the envelopes and saved in an envelope for the major. He's an avid collector of foreign stamps and claims to have the biggest stamp collection in Wiltshire.'

I put a concerned look on my face. 'Well, I might have thrown a few away because they were damaged. He wouldn't want those, would he? Anyway, why all the fuss, we receive loads of stamps every day and lots of them are the same.'

'That's all very well, but they all have value and the major likes to have stamps he can exchange with other philatelists. He might even sell some of the more valuable and sought after ones. The major expects us to have some stamps for his collection whenever he calls into the office. Just be more careful in future.'

'I will, I certainly will,' I promised gravely, 'but what's a *philatelist*, when he's at home?' I asked.

'A philatelist is a stamp collector. I'm surprised that you didn't know that. Didn't you ever save stamps? Most boys do, if not stamps, foreign coins, cigarette cards or some such trivia,' replied Humbledick in an impatient tone.

'No, I've never saved stamps, but I do save film star photographs. I send away to Hollywood for them. I've got dozens, including: Edward G Robinson, George Raft, Betty Grable, Paul Henreid, Franchot Tone, Deanna Durbin, Claire Trevor, Humphrey Bogart, Errol Flynn, Joan Crawford, John Garfield, James Stewart, Randolph Scott, Ingrid

Bergman, Bette Davis, John Wayne, Esther Williams, Peter Lorre and lots, lots more,' I said with pride.

'*Peter Lorre*! Why would anyone want a photograph of that ugly little Hungarian?' asked Humbledick.

'Because he is a good actor and has been in some smashing films, such as *The Island of Doomed Men, The Maltese Falcon, Casablanca, Passage to Marseilles, The Mask of Dimitrios*,' I catalogued in defence of my choice of unlikely heroes. '"Rick, Rick help me, please help me, hide me, you must do something, Rick…"' I parodied, in what friends had told me was a pretty good imitation of the voice of Peter Lorre. 'Doesn't that sound just like him? It was a line from the film *Casablanca*. I also do some of his lines from *The Maltese Falcon*, but I have a friend with strange, staring eyes, just like Peter Lorre's, who can imitate his voice so well you'd think it actually was the actor speaking.'

'Oh, very good, indeed,' said Humbledick, with unrestrained sarcasm. 'Which only goes to show that you spend far too much time in the cinema when what you ought to be doing is something worthwhile, like going to night school to take a course in office practice or a foreign language.'

I didn't answer him; I was too busy thinking of what he had said about the foreign stamps having *value*. That was something I needed to look into at the first opportunity.

CHAPTER 6

▼

Next day, while Charles Humbledick was out to lunch, I browsed the London *Telephone Directory*, in search of philatelists and stamp dealers. My search quickly revealed the whereabouts of the nearest stamp dealer, a Morris Mossoff, who had a stamp and coin shop in Fenchurch Street, not more than five minutes walk from the office. I knew it would be unwise to risk leaving the office while Humbledick was out as the major had instructed that it must be 'manned' during our opening times and it would be just like him to telephone the office to see if someone was there to answer the phone. So, after I had finished my spam sandwiches and bottle of ginger beer lunch, I gathered together the foreign stamps I had collected from the day's post and, after sorting them into two even piles, placed them into two envelopes—one to be saved for the major's next visit, and one for me to take to the dealer the next day.

With a bit of luck I might get some cash for the weekend. I needed enough to pay for two cinema tickets, a couple of tubs of ice cream, 20 fags and a trolleybus ride home. Five bob should cover it.

I wasn't planning to take a girlfriend to the cinema, I didn't have one, but since I didn't like going on my own, I would take my between-jobs pal, Cyril Magwick. I felt sure that he would do the same for me if he was working and I was unemployed. Well, that's what pals are for, isn't it?

Stamps, coins and medals—bought and sold, I read on the window of Morris Mossoff's shop. I entered, trying to look worldly, with knowledge of philately. It didn't work on this geezer.

'Yes, sonny, what can I do for you?'

No 'good morning, sir', not a very good start, I thought.

'You do buy foreign stamps, don't you?' I asked unnecessarily.

'That's what it says on my window,' came the dealer's sarcastic reply.

This wasn't going well at all. I felt like giving up and trying somewhere else, but I pulled my brown envelope out of my jacket pocket and laid it on the counter.

'I want to sell these stamps. Would you be interested in buying them?'

Mossoff sniffed, picked up the envelope and spilled its contents onto the counter, and then, taking up an oversized pair of tweezers, he started to turn the stamps face up and place them into three piles. 'There's not much here that's any use to me. Some are damaged and you've cut off too much of the envelope. You should leave about a quarter of an inch all around the stamp. A few of these South American stamps are worth a few coppers, but as to the rest, they'd have to be sold in packets. I'll tell you what, I'll give you three shillings for the lot and chance losing on the deal.'

'Three bob, is that *all*? I was hoping they might be worth about five shillings.'

'Not a chance, old son, but tell me, do you work in an office that gets lots of foreign mail?'

'Yes, I do, I work in a ship chandler's agent's office,' I replied, sensing that Mossoff was, perhaps, more interested in my stamps than he wanted to let on.

'Well, son, if you could bring me a regular supply of stamps once a month, I might be inclined to look more favourably on what you've got here, and stretch it to four shillings, but that's my absolute limit.'

I pretended to mull over his offer, but not for too long. 'Yes, I could do that. I'll make it the last Friday in the month to come in,' I said, trying to sound business-like.

'That'll suit me,' Mossoff replied.

'Oh, Mr Mossoff, I wonder if you've got some sort of list or catalogue that gives the value of stamps? If I had one I could make sure that I only bring in the higher valued ones.'

Mossoff laughed. 'Ha, so you are taking a real interest in stamps, are you? The cheapest catalogue I have would cost you five and six. Too much for you, I'm sure, but I like to see young people taking an interest in stamps, so I'll let you have this second-hand catalogue for sixpence. It's a 1936 catalogue, and the more modern stamps will not be included in it, but it'll help you to gain more knowledge about stamps.'

'Thanks, I'll buy it.'

'So, I now owe you three and sixpence,' Mossoff said, as he opened his cash box, took out some coins and handed me a half-crown and a shilling.

'Thanks, and cheerio,' I said, as I pocketed the money and left the shop. 'I'll be in at the end of September with some more stamps.'

'Goodbye, lad,' Mossoff called out as I closed the door.

Not as much as I had hoped to raise, but I now had a stamp catalogue to study and the three and six would get me two, one and threepenny cinema tickets and twenty Player's Weights. Things could be a lot worse.

CHAPTER 7

▼

During a rare slack period in the office, Humbledick went out to buy some pipe tobacco. He usually sent me out to get it for him, but after I had forgotten to give him his change on a couple of occasions, he decided to get it himself.

I was struggling to complete the previous day's *Evening News* crossword puzzle. Giving up on the puzzle, I got to thinking about girls. I hadn't had a proper date for months. The only girl that I had ever taken a real fancy to was one of my classmates in my last year at school. I had asked her to go swimming with me in the Danson Park open-air swimming pool on the Sunday. It didn't cost much to get in, and I would get to see a lot more of the girl. At first she agreed, but on the Friday she cried off, saying: 'I'm afraid I can't come swimming with you on Sunday.'

'Why not?' I asked her. 'The weather is supposed to be very hot and sunny this weekend.'

'Well…er…I've got to wash my hair,' she replied lamely.

I persisted with my request, but she wouldn't change her mind. It was several months after we had both left school that she met me and apologised for breaking the date because she had had one of those 'girlie problems'.

'You mean you had your *period*,' I said with unnecessary frankness.

She was so appalled by my 'insensitivity', as she put it, that I realised I had little chance of forming any sort of relationship with her.

My first date with a girl was unforgettable. What was her name? Oh yes, I remember, it was Pearl, Pearl Thwaites. I'd promised to call on her one evening in the summer of 1944 and my former school friend and henchman, Cyril Magwick, had accompanied me. He had little interest in girls and wouldn't prove to be any competition, so I didn't mind him playing the 'gooseberry' on this occasion.

When we arrived at Pearl's home, situated near the Royal Artillery Barracks on Woolwich Common, Pearl answered the door.

'Oh, it's you, Archie. I'm sorry, I forgot that you were coming tonight. I'm afraid I can't come out with you. I'm washing my hair and my sister has come over especially to set it for me,' explained Pearl, in a matter-of-fact tone.

Washing her hair! Is that the only excuse a girl can come up with? As it was clear that Pearl was not going to invite me in, I thought I'd keep her talking in the porch, possibly even get her to change her mind. Cyril was discreetly out of sight of Pearl, sitting on the next door's front garden wall smoking, but no doubt listening to every word we said.

'Do you really have to wash your hair tonight? Wouldn't you rather come out for a walk on the common with me? Or, if you'd rather, we could still make the last house at the Globe Cinema?' I said, in my most appealing tone.

Pearl hesitated slightly before she replied. 'No…er…I'm afraid not. I can't let my sister down as she's come all the way from Sidcup to do my hair. Anyway, my dad doesn't like me to be out at night with boys he doesn't know. I'd ask you in to meet my family, but as I've said, I'm washing my hair and by the time it has dried and my sister has set it for me, it'll be time for bed. Can't we make it some other time?'

I smiled as if I wasn't bothered about her refusal, but I was disappointed and not a little angry. Pearl had agreed to go out with me days ago and now she was giving me the runaround.

'OK, perhaps we can get together next week to go out for an afternoon—'

I was interrupted by the unmistakable sound of a doodlebug's engine as it approached overhead. I pushed Pearl back into her hallway and shouted: 'Quick Pearl, get under your Morrison shelter!'

'We haven't got one!' Pearl answered with a trace of panic in her voice.

'Then get in the under stairs cupboard!' I shouted back at her as I left the porch to join Cyril on the pavement. 'Let's get the hell out of here!' I shouted as I ran down the street looking for somewhere to shelter.

Cyril needed no prompting and was right on my heels as we both raced the length of the street. I remembered there was a bombsite at the bottom, where several houses had been demolished and the area partially cleared of debris. In the middle of the site was a fairly deep crater, filled with brick, rubble and water. The flying bomb's engine suddenly stopped and the unmanned aircraft went into a slow glide, skimming the chimney pots and turning towards us again as it descended. Breathlessly, we reached the crater and hurled ourselves into it, to lie in a state of sheer panic, amid the submerged rubble. Seconds later the doodlebug glided rooftop height above us, to crash with a huge explosion amidst the barrack's hutted accommodation area, killing, as we were to hear later, several ATS girls. Shaking, scratched, bruised and soaking wet, we scrambled from the crater and limped home.

I never called upon Pearl Thwaites again. Her preference for her sister's attention to her hair rather than an outing with me, coupled with my near-death experience with the doodlebug, put me off girls for a bit, but not for very long.

My thoughts were suddenly disturbed. I sensed I was being watched. There was nobody else in the office so perhaps the window cleaner was outside on his cradle, looking in through the window. I looked out—he wasn't. I glanced up to the next-door, third floor window, and saw a girl staring down into the office. She must be looking at me, I thought, and as I looked up at her she slowly turned away from the window, probably embarrassed that she had been seen.

When Humbledick returned to the office I told him about the girl's apparent interest in our office.

'She was looking down at *you*? She probably fancies you. You weren't doing something you didn't ought to do, were you?' he asked suggestively.

'Of course not, I was finishing off the amendments to Henry Risgalla's Port Said price list. Watermelons have gone up .75 of a piastre,' I said, hoping to add some credibility to my statement.

*   *   *   *

During the week that followed I made a point of frequently glancing up at the third floor window. More often than not the girl was standing at the window and gazing down into our office. From what I could make out about her, at the distance between us, was that she was a brunette and appeared to be quite attractive. I decided that it was time for me to make my move. As soon as Humbledick left the office to go to the toilet, I looked up at the window until the girl appeared. As soon as she did, I indicated with hand signals that she should come down to my floor. She nodded her head and raised her hand to signal five minutes with her fingers.

As soon as Humbledick returned, I excused myself to go to the lavatory. I walked to the end of the corridor and stood at the top of the staircase, opposite the lift. A minute or so later the girl stepped out of the lift. Basil Bates, the liftman, gave a knowing grin as he saw me step forwards. I waited until the lift had descended out of sight before I spoke.

'Hello, my name is Archie Cholmondeley, what's yours?' I said, with a broad smile to display my even white teeth. That always impressed and sometimes evoked a flattering comment from girls, who seemed more concerned about such physical attributes.

'My name is Daphne Weldunn,' she replied with a smile.

Not bad, I thought, not bad at all. The girl was a little less than average height and her mid-brown hair was set in the 'pageboy' style. Her face was oval shaped and her eyes were hazel coloured. She was nicely rounded, her firm young breasts thrusting outwards, as though straining to free themselves from the restriction of a too small a cup size brassiere. Her legs were well shaped and enhanced by very hard-to-come-by nylon stockings, which seemed out of character with the rest of her apparel. Perhaps she'd been friendly with a Yank, although she didn't look the type who would swap her favours for a pair of stockings.

'I thought it was about time we met properly, rather than keep staring at each other through windows,' I said with a laugh. 'I work for Keith Carlton-Smythe; he's a ship chandler's agent.'

She looked puzzled, but didn't ask for an explanation. 'My firm deals with maritime insurance. It's all very boring; that's why I keep looking out of the window.'

'Look, I'll have to get back to my office now, or my boss will think I've had a nasty accident in the lavatory,' I said, hoping she wouldn't be put off me by my spontaneous, but lame, joke. 'But I'd like to meet you when we pack up for the day. Perhaps we could go to the ABC for some tea. Can you meet me at the entrance at about four thirty?'

'Yes, I'd like that,' she said enthusiastically.

'Till four thirty then,' I said, as I turned to head back to my office and she took to the stairs.

*   *   *   *

She was waiting just inside the main door of the building as I came down the staircase. She was wearing a heavy winter's coat, a beret and a thick woollen scarf around her neck. She looked like a third year student on a school outing to visit the sights of London. She gave a coy smile as I approached.

'You haven't been waiting long, have you?' I asked, not because I was particularly concerned, but it seemed the right thing to say.

'No, I've just got here. It's very cold outside. Is that thin raincoat you're wearing warm enough for this weather?' she asked, seeming to be genuinely concerned.

'Yes, it's fine, I don't feel the cold; here, feel this,' I said, as I extended my right hand.

She grasped my hand with a hand that was soft and cool.

'Oh, yes, your hands are warm. Are you like that all over?'

'Yes, I am. As a matter of fact, some say I'm pretty hot stuff.'

She blushed slightly and gave an embarrassed laugh at my hackneyed innuendo. So she was prudish.

'Well, we'd better be getting a move on if we are to get some tea before I have to catch my train at six,' I said, as I took her arm and ushered her through the swing doors and out onto the pavement.

The ABC was nearly empty. I selected a corner table and helped her off with her coat.

'Tea and scones all right for you?' I asked, as I started for the counter.

'Yes, tea will be fine, but no scones for me; my dinner will be waiting for me when I get home,' she replied.

'Yes, I expect mine will be as well, so I'll follow your example and forgo the scones.'

I brought the tea back to the table—no waitress service in the ABC. I preferred it that way; waitresses always expected a tip. We talked about interests, our hobbies and ourselves, our jobs and our homes. I learned that she was nearly 18, but didn't look it and that she had never had a boyfriend. I told her I was 18 and was waiting to be called up for national service. She said she had an older brother who was in the army, serving in Palestine. She lived in Ponders End and I laughed at that, never having believed there was such a place in London. I told her I lived in Woolwich. 'The bottom right-hand corner of London,' I added, with a laugh.

I offered her a cigarette. She said she didn't smoke. Too bad, I thought, but refrained from lighting up. She shared my keen interest in the cinema and was clearly impressed when I told her of my hobby of collecting autographed film star photographs. I promised to take my collection into work one day to show her.

'Speaking of film stars, would you like to go to the cinema with me?' I asked.

'Yes, that would be nice. Have you a particular film in mind?'

'Yes, I have, it's a new film, *The Lost Weekend*, and it's showing at the Dominion Cinema, Tottenham Court Road. Ray Milland and Jane Wyman are the stars. It's very highly rated and Ray Milland has been tipped to win the best actor Oscar for his performance as an alcoholic writer,' I said with enthusiasm.

Her expression told me she was not very keen on my choice of film.

'It doesn't sound like the sort of film I would enjoy, but Ray Milland is quite a good actor. He played a good part in *Beau Geste*, and I rather like Jane Wyman. Isn't she married to that cowboy actor, Ronald Reagan?'

'Yes, I believe she is,' I said, thinking, this girl knows almost as much about films stars as I do. 'So, that's settled then, we'll seek out *The Lost Weekend*, this weekend. We can meet on Saturday, outside the underground station, at about one o'clock. That'll put us right to catch the first performance.'

'Sounds perfect,' Daphne enthused, 'and to round off our day, I'd like to invite you for tea at my home. We'll be out of the cinema at about four and can catch a bus, which stops a few yards from my home.'

I didn't much care for family tea parties, but having a meal at the Weldunn's would save me having to buy one in town, which Daphne would probably expect me to do before we went home.

'That'll be nice, I'll look forward to meeting your family,' I lied.

'Lovely, I'm sure you'll get on with my mother. I didn't mention it before, but she is separated from my father. You won't see him as he's living up north somewhere with the woman he left home for.'

'Oh, I'm sorry to hear that,' I said, with genuine sympathy. I knew, only too well what life could be like without a father.

'Oh, my brothers and I were not a bit sorry to see him go. He was beastly to mother. He drank too much, gambled on slow horses and chased everything in skirts.'

I put on a serious face. 'It must have been awful for the family.'

'Yes, it was and I vowed that I'd never get involved with anyone like him.'

'So, I'll see you at one o'clock, on Saturday at the Tottenham Court Road tube station, Daphne,' I said, determined to change the subject as we left the ABC.

'Yes, and in the meantime I'll be keeping an eye on you from my window on the third floor,' she said with a laugh.

CHAPTER 8

▼

'Where are you off to, all spruced up?' my mother asked as I was leaving the house to catch a train to London.

'If you must know, I've a date in town with a gorgeous brunette. We're going to see *The Lost Weekend*, at the Dominion Cinema and afterwards, Daphne—that's her name—has invited me to her home in Ponders End, for tea with her family.'

'Having tea with her family on the first date, eh? You'll be getting engaged next. Just remember, you might look like a man, but you're not 16 until next month.'

'Goodbye, Mum, see you about midnight—if you're still up,' I said with a laugh as I closed the front door.

*　　　*　　　*　　　*

Daphne was waiting just inside the entrance to the underground station. We exchanged smiles as I approached her.

'It's not far to walk from here to the cinema.'

'I know,' she agreed, as she took my arm.

I wasn't used to girls holding my arm. It made me feel that the girl had some sort of hold over me, and that was something for which I was unprepared.

Arriving at the cinema, I took out my Egyptian leather wallet (a homecoming present from my 'desert rat' uncle) as I approached the booking office, and withdrew a ten-shilling note.

'Two four and sixes, please.'

The cashier worked her machine and gave me the tickets and my shilling change.

Settled in our seats, waiting for the lights to go down and the *Pathe News, Time Marches On,* or the trailer of a forthcoming film to appear, I took off my raincoat and spread it across our knees.

'It's not very warm in here because of the draughts, but my coat should keep the draughts off your legs.'

Daphne turned to me and whispered, 'You'd better make sure that everything else of yours is kept off my legs.'

I grinned sheepishly and gave her hand a gentle squeeze. 'I promise to behave myself like a gentleman,' I whispered.

Before Daphne could answer, the curtains went up and the loud introduction of the *Pathe News* prevented further conversation.

During the film I lost myself in Ray Milland's interpretation of the alcoholic writer's lost weekend and trying to imagine what it would be like to become so drunk that your mental processes would inspire words such as:

> *Suddenly I am above the ordinary. I'm competent, supremely competent. I'm walking a tightrope over Niagara Falls. I'm one of the great ones. I'm Michelangelo moulding the beard of Moses. I'm Van Gogh, painting pure sunlight. I'm Horowitz, playing the Emperor Concerto. I'm Jesse James and his two brothers, all three of them. I'm William Shakespeare…*

I was suddenly aware of Daphne tugging at my arm and whispering, 'Archie, let me pass, please, I want to go to the toilet.'

I removed my raincoat from her knees and stood up to let her pass. My little ploy with the raincoat had been all to no avail, but it didn't matter, I was enjoying the film. During her unduly long absence I lit a cigarette and recalled the only time that I had been drunk; I had been given two or three glasses of neat whisky by a tipsy relative who was celebrating VE day. During my period of resultant drunkenness, I had no recollection of expounding any profound or meaningful words like those I had just heard uttered by the character in the film. I had simply been as sick as a dog that had eaten bad meat.

Daphne returned and eased herself by me to her seat, whispering as she did, 'I'm sorry I was such a long time, I've got a bit of a tummy upset.'

I took the hint and didn't bother to cover our knees with my raincoat.

Waiting at a bus stop for a bus to take us to Ponders End, I asked, 'Did you enjoy the film?'

'Well, yes, it was rather good acting on the part of Ray Milland, but the scenes in the alcoholic ward were terrible. Do people really carry on like that when they have had too much to drink? I wouldn't want to be married or have anything to do with someone who got in that state.'

I was saved having to come up with an answer by the arrival of our bus.

Arriving at Daphne's house, she rang the doorbell. Nearly 18 and doesn't have a door key, I thought. An unkempt and cheeky faced boy, who I was later to learn was Daphne's 12-year-old brother, answered the door.

'Oh, it's you, Daffy. Is he your boyfriend? He's big, isn't he?' Turning to me, he went on, 'If you are, you're the first she's had.'

'Don't be rude, Tommy, and I've told you a thousand times, not to call me Daffy. This is Mr Archibald Cholmondeley, a friend. We work in neighbouring buildings. Please show Mr Cholmondeley where to hang his coat.'

I handed Tommy my coat. 'You can call me Archie, Tommy,' I said with a wink.

Mrs Weldunn appeared in the hall, wearing a smile of welcome. Daphne introduced me to her mother, a short, dumpy, pudding-faced woman, with frizzy reddish hair, probably dyed, I thought. Mrs Weldunn looked up at me admiringly. 'You *are* a tall young man. He's taller than your brother, Daphne. You look old enough to be in the army, Archie. When do you get called up?'

'Pretty soon,' I lied, 'but I don't fancy the army with all their "bull". I'm going to try to get into the RAF.'

'Does that mean you'll be a pilot?' asked Mrs Weldunn excitedly.

'That's hardly likely, as I've not got the educational qualifications to be accepted for aircrew. Anyway, I'm not all that keen on the idea of flying. Few people realise it, but for everyone who flies in the RAF, there are about 50 airmen and airwomen on the ground in support,' I said, with the authority of someone who had read all the pamphlets in the local recruiting office.

'For your sake, one thing I hope is that they don't cut off all your lovely, wavy, brown hair, which nicely matches your eyes. My son, Edward, looked awful after his first haircut in the army,' said Mrs Weldunn. 'I must say that you do keep it very well groomed. What sort of hairdressing cream do you use to keep it that way?'

Before I could answer, Tommy interrupted.

'I bet it's Brylcreem. Edward says that all the RAF bods are a bunch of sissies who use Brylcreem to keep their long hair in place. They copy that smarmy cricketer. You know the bloke I'm talking about, what's-his-name—he advertises Brylcreem.'

'No, I don't use Brycreem; I make my own hair oil from a mixture of liquid paraffin and tragacanth. One of my mother's lodgers gave me the recipe.'

Tommy looked at me in awe. 'You mean you make your—'

I cut him short. 'The man you are talking about, who advertises Brylcreem, is Dennis Compton, one of the best batsmen we've had in the England team for years. He's a great all-round sportsman. He also plays football for Arsenal,' I sharply interposed.

'Yeah, that's the geezer I'm on about, he—'

'Oh, do be quiet, Tommy, you're being very rude to Mr Cholmondeley,' said Mrs Weldunn. 'I've told you often enough that you shouldn't argue with your elders, who know better than you. In any case, I think Dennis Compton is a very handsome, dashing young man. He is also a fine role model for our youngsters to follow, and as for calling RAF men sissy Brylcreem boys, I can't think what your brother was thinking about. Surely he must remember how courageously they fought in the Battle of Britain.'

'But, Mum—'

'That's enough, Tommy. Not another word about it,' snapped Mrs Weldunn. She turned to us, a smile replacing her scowl. 'Children, tea is now ready,' she said, and ushered us into the dining room. 'I hope you'll like it, Archie; it's so difficult with rationing to make enjoyable meals these days. I expect your mother has the same problem.'

I nodded and smiled.

'Anyway, I've made bloater paste and cucumber sandwiches, and spam fritters; there's home-made blackberry jam, seed cake, rock cakes, fairy cakes and fruit junket and jelly.'

'Sounds like a feast fit for a king,' I said, to please her.

She beamed. 'You sit at the head of the table, Archie. Tommy, leave those cakes alone and get upstairs and wash your hands and face before you sit at the table.'

The four of us sat around the table. There was little conversation. Daphne delicately nibbled her sandwiches; Mrs Weldunn held her tea-cup with her small finger stuck out while Tommy ate his food like he'd been starved for a week.

Mrs Weldunn wanted to hear all about the film we had seen. Daphne gave a brief summary of it, leaving out the more lurid scenes of drunkenness, no doubt believing that the contents of a film given an 'A' certificate should not be told to a child of under 16 years. Tommy, with blackcurrant jam covering most of his mouth and chin, sat in rapt attention throughout.

'So what's an alcoholic?' he asked.

'Someone who drinks too much and is always drunk,' simplified Daphne.

'So you didn't like it very much then, Daphne?' queried Mrs Weldunn, as she refilled her teacup.

'Oh, it was all right, I suppose. Anyway, Archie seemed to enjoy it.'

I nodded, in agreement.

'They don't make films like they used to,' interposed Mrs Weldunn. 'I remember the wonderful films that were made before the talkies came in; films with Douglas Fairbanks, Mary Pickford, Lillian Gish, Gilbert Roland, Gloria Swanson and Rudolph Valentino—such wonderful actors.'

I stifled a yawn. 'Yes, I'm sure they were, Mrs Weldunn, but it's better now that they can talk on the screen and you don't have to guess what they are supposed to be saying.'

Mrs Weldunn looked hurt and changed the subject. 'What are your career plans, Archie? What will you do when you've finished your national service? Have you any future intentions about settling down and getting married?'

Getting married! I gulped. What was she on about? I had momentarily forgotten I was supposed to be 18 and would be over 20 when I finished my national service, an age when, because of the war, many people had got married. 'I don't know what I'll do, but I'd like to get a job with a newspaper. If I can't get that I might join the police force, but it's much too early for me to be thinking about marriage, I'm—'

'Can I leave the table, Mum?' interrupted Tommy as he snatched the last rock cake from the table, jumped off his chair and left the room.

Mrs Weldunn didn't answer but just glowered briefly before returning to our conversation. 'The police force, you say, that's a good career—carries a very good pension. My son, Edward, is due to come out of the army soon and he's thinking of going into the police. Well, the Palestine police. He's based in Jerusalem at the moment and has a Jewish girlfriend. He says the government are desperately trying to recruit more police for the force. They must be expecting a lot of trouble with all the Jewish people trying to get back to Palestine.'

'Mum, Archie doesn't want to hear all about the problems of Palestine and Edward's plans for the future. I'll clear the table and get Tommy to bring his Ludo down and then the four of us can have a game. We haven't played for months, not since Edward was on embarkation leave.'

'Now that is a really good idea, Daphne. Yes, I'm sure Archie would prefer to do that rather than talking about family affairs.'

This was getting worse. Playing *Ludo* with the Weldunn's? I could think of nothing more depressingly boring. 'I'd love to play Ludo, but I really must be leaving soon. I've promised to go to my grandmother's tomorrow to do some painting for her and want to make an early start, which means getting to bed reasonably early tonight, and I have got well over an hour's journey to get home. Thank you very much for the lovely tea, Mrs Weldunn. It's been a great evening, one I'm sure I'll not forget.' I said, as I arose from my chair and moved to leave the room.

'Oh, what a pity, I thought you'd be stopping until ten o'clock, at least. Never mind, perhaps you could come again for tea, even stay the weekend. I'm sure we could find something interesting for you to do while you were here. Still, you are a good lad, helping your grandmother. She must be very proud, having a grandson like you.'

I coloured up, embarrassed and feeling guilty; the excuse I'd made, necessary as it was, had come to mind too easily. 'Oh, that's nothing special, doing a bit of painting,' I said in a contrite tone. 'I was always brought up to respect and help the elderly and infirm.'

Daphne brought my coat from the hall. I slipped it on and she followed me to the front door. Mrs Weldunn called out, 'Goodbye Archie,' from the dining room door, 'I hope to see you here again, soon.'

'Goodbye, Mrs Weldunn,' I replied, with resigned finality.

I stood on the doorstep with Daphne, at a loss as to what to say. She was attracted to me, of that there was no doubt, and she was pretty in a sort of elfin way; her figure had the curves in the right places, but her attitudes and responses seemed almost childlike. Instead of being two years older than me, she seemed to be that much younger. No wonder she'd never had a boyfriend. She was boring and, as far as I could ascertain from my short time with her, had little sex appeal, or any real desire to try to develop any. In other words, to put it bluntly, although her equipment was in good order, she was reluctant to put it into operation.

'Well, goodnight Daphne, I guess I'll see you around Lloyds Avenue, from time to time,' I said, grasping her hand and shaking it.

She leaned forwards, her head raised and her lips pursed as though expecting me to kiss her. It seemed the right thing to do so I caught her up in my arms and gave her a passionate French kiss. There was little response and her breath smelled fishy. Something, out of deference to her, I had avoided, by not eating the bloater paste sandwiches.

CHAPTER 9

▼

After my disappointing, if not disastrous, date with Daphne, the first thing I did when I got to the office on Monday was to move my desk nearer the window. It left a smaller space between Mr Humbledick's desk and mine.

'I find the light is not very good in the centre of the room,' I explained, when Mr Humbledick questioned my move.

He raised no objection—perhaps he guessed the real reason for my move.

My new position in the office made it impossible for me to be seen from the third floor next door. Occasionally, when I was standing near the filing cabinets, I would take a sly peek up at the window. Whenever I did, she was standing at the window. Daphne kept up her vigil at the window for about two weeks, after which she suddenly appeared no more. Perhaps she's left for another job, I thought, or been moved to another office. It didn't occur to me that she might now have a boy-friend and, therefore, no longer wished to carry a torch for me.

I had other fish to fry. My foreign stamp fiddle was not netting as much as it had been as we were getting fewer letters and more cable-grams. Stamps were becoming scarce, and because of the major's growing suspicion—'Is that all you've got for me this week?'—that I might be keeping them for my 'own collection', I was obliged to put more stamps into his envelope. It got to the point that it was hardly worth a visit to Mossoff's shop with so few stamps.

'You'll have to do better than this,' Mossoff said, as he turned over my latest offering of about a dozen commonplace stamps of little value. 'They're not worth the time I spend looking at them.'

'OK, Mr Mossoff, I'll not call in unless I've got 50 or more stamps to sell.'

'Suit yourself, Archie, but what I really want to get my hands on are full sets of stamps, particularly African and Asian. Get me those and I'll pay you well.'

Fortune must have been smiling on me, for it was barely a week later, when opening a letter from our principal in Kuala Lumpur, that I found that the envelope contained two full sets of every value of unused Malaya stamps. The letter was typewritten in understandable English. Its writer had probably been educated in a British university. I read it carefully, to see if there was any reference in it to indicate that *two* sets of stamps were enclosed. There was none. All that was written about them was: '…knowing how much you like to collect foreign stamps, I thought you might like these new issue stamps for your collection…'

This was a real coup. I couldn't wait to get the stamps to Mossoff. I carefully cut the stamp from the envelope, and placed it, together with a single set of the mint stamps, in the envelope. I clipped the envelope to the letter and filed it in the Kuala Lumpur file. This, I felt, would ensure that when the major read the letter, he wouldn't need to query what stamps the letter had contained. I placed the second set of stamps in a clean envelope and put them in the inside pocket of my raincoat, ready to take to Mossoff at lunchtime. I then set to with a smile on my face as I opened and filed the rest of the mail before Mr Humbledick arrived.

'You look pleased with yourself this morning, Archie. Did you manage to get your oats with Daphne over the weekend?' asked Humbledick with unaccustomed vulgar familiarity as he started to read the morning's mail I had laid out on his desk.

'No, that little romance wasn't going anywhere and is now well and truly over. I haven't seen her since I took her to the cinema and suffered a tea party with her mother and younger brother. They even tried to get me to play *Ludo*!' I exclaimed, at the same time thinking of an excuse for my obviously happy mood. 'Actually, my grandmother has sent me a pound postal order for my birthday. She's a bit early, but then she's always getting names and dates muddled.'

'How generous of your grandmother. I bet you'll be straight around to the post office at lunchtime to cash your postal order,' said Humbledick with a wide grin.

'I certainly will and I expect I'll have lunch in the ABC today to celebrate,' I replied with undisguised smugness.

'My, my, the major will be pleased when he sees this set of stamps Mr Kandalia has sent him from Kuala Lumpur!' exclaimed Humbledick as he read the letter from our Malayan principal. 'High-priced Malaya stamps like this must be worth quite a lot to an English collector.'

'Yes, I suppose they would be,' I replied, trying to sound disinterested.

*   *   *   *

'Now *these* are more like what I want,' said Mossoff, almost drooling over the Malaya stamps as he examined them.

'So, these will be worth a tidy packet, will they?' I asked, trying to imagine what he would pay me for them.

'Well, they're certainly the best you've brought in, but I don't know what they'll raise on the open market. I'll have to think about it. Of course, they are mint stamps and anyone could send to Malaya to buy a set.'

I didn't like the way the deal was going. I sensed that Mossoff was out to make himself a nice profit at my expense.

'But the country's only recently been liberated from the Japanese, so there can't be many current Malaya stamps about. The Malayans weren't writing to Britain during the war, were they?' I said, with unrestrained sarcasm.

'Well, since it's you, I'll risk losing on the deal. I'll give you 50 per cent of their face value in Malaya. How's that?'

'I don't know, and neither do you, until we find out from the bank what Malay currency is worth in this country,' I retorted.

'What about a tenner, then?' suggested Mossoff in a conciliatory tone.

A tenner—what does he mean, ten shillings? He surely can't mean ten pounds, or can he? Well, ten pounds were referred to as a tenner, weren't they, I mused. I decided to take the risk.

'OK, it's a deal, ten quid for the set,' I said, with uneasy assurance.

Mossoff carefully placed the stamps in a cardboard folder and put the folder under the counter. 'I won't be a minute,' he said. 'I'll have to get the money from my safe.'

He retired through a curtained doorway into a back room. I waited, excitedly planning what I could buy with ten pounds. It was more money than I had ever had in my life. It was almost six weeks' wages working for Major Carlton-Smythe. I put on a serious expression when he returned to the shop. He was clutching a large—well, it seemed large to me—bundle of rather old and scruffy looking pound and ten shillings notes. 'Ten pounds was what we agreed, eh?'

My mouth was dry, I couldn't speak; I nodded agreement.

'One, two, three, four, five, six, seven, eight, nine, ten,' he said, as he laid the notes one on top of the other on the counter.

I stared at the untidy little pile of pound notes for several seconds.

'Well, they're yours. Pick them up, before I change my mind,' Mossoff barked.

I snatched the notes from the counter, took my wallet out of my inside jacket pocket and quickly pushed the bundle into the wallet.

'Thanks and cheerio, Mr Mossoff!' I shouted as I hurriedly left the shop.

My first port of call on my way back to the office was to a tobacconist.

'Twenty Peter Stuyvesant and an ounce of St Julian pipe tobacco, please,' I said, peeling off one of my pound notes and placing it on the counter.

*   *   *   *

Back at the office, Mr Humbledick was sitting at his desk reading the *Daily Chronicle* while he munched cheese and pickle sandwiches and drank tea from his vacuum flask lid. He looked up when I entered the office. 'I bet that pound note was burning a hole in your pocket,' he said with a laugh. 'What did you buy with it?'

'Just some fags, and this is for you,' I said, as I dropped the packet of tobacco on his desk.

Humbledick looked puzzled. 'What's this in aid of?' he asked.

'Think of it as a belated Christmas present,' I replied.

'Well, thanks very much, it's very kind of you, but you shouldn't spend your money on the likes of me. If you've nothing to spend it on for yourself, save it for a rainy day.'

'That's my trouble—it's always a rainy day for me,' I said, as I unwrapped the Peter Stuyvesants and lit one with my US flip-top lighter.

CHAPTER 10

▼

The ten pounds didn't last me long. I had a brown pinstriped suit made at the Fifty Shilling Tailors, and bought a couple of shirts, a pair of shoes and some socks. That was more than half the money spent and my annual quota of clothing coupons exhausted. I bought my mother a box of 50 Player's Weights, Eddie, my carpenter stepfather, a quarter inch wood chisel and our lodger, Dennis Wallow, 20 Senior Service. The rest I spent on a blowout of pies, peas and mash for my in-between-jobs mate, Cyril Magwick, and myself at Manzies Eel and Pie Shop, followed by an afternoon in the local bug hutch watching a Wild Bill Elliott western, while we smoked the best part of a packet of Passing Cloud cigarettes and flirted, to no avail, with the two girls who were sitting in front of us.

What the ten pounds had done was to give me a taste of high living—something I was determined to continue.

I was preparing the major's annual letter for dispatch to all our overseas principals. Copies of the various contracts the major had negotiated with the shipowners, on behalf of the ship chandlers we represented, accompanied the letter. The letters needed to be sent airmail and because of the high cost of airmail postage, each letter had to be carefully weighed to ascertain the exact amount of postage it required to reach its destination.

Mr Humbledick had warned me: 'Always make sure that the postage is correct for the weight sent. We don't want to upset any of our principals by causing them to have to pay a surcharge on the letters they receive from us.'

It was remembering this instruction that got me thinking. Suppose the scales were faulty and they registered incorrect weights, by either increasing or decreasing the weight of the letter, depending which side of the scales was faulty?

While I was alone in the office over the lunch break, I experimented with my theory by placing additional items, a few paper clips or an empty cigarette packet, first on the side upon which the letter was placed, then on the side of the scales that bore the weights. When the additional items were placed on the letter plate, the scales balanced slightly over the normal weight of our letters, about half an ounce, which required one and threepence worth of postage stamps. By registering the weight fractionally higher it meant that the letter would appear to require the one-ounce rate, amounting to two and sixpence worth of stamps. When the additional weight was placed with the weights, it registered the letter's weight as being below the one ounce level, but that was purely of academic interest for my concern was how I could doctor the scales to overweigh mail and yet, when examined, they would appear to be working correctly. What I needed was something I could quickly attach to the underside of the letter plate and when all the letters for dispatch had been weighed, remove it quickly so that the scales would be correct when anyone else used them.

I sat at my desk and pondered the problem. A cigarette would help, but I had smoked my last one on the train that morning. A couple of pieces of chewing gum would have to console me while I chewed over the problem of the scales. That was it—simple! I would chew some gum while I was weighing the mail. When Humbledick, or anybody else who was in the office, wasn't looking I would quickly stick the gum under the letter plate and pencil the higher airmail postage rate on the overweighted envelopes. As was my usual practice, I would add up the postage required for the letters and Humbledick would give me the exact amount to pay for the stamps at the local post office.

This turned out to be one of my most lucrative fiddles. It kept me in cigarettes, ABC lunches and regular visits to the cinema, and also enabled me to add some new clothes to my wardrobe, which, with clothes rationing and my clothing coupon sales to Mrs Carl-ton-Smythe, had mainly comprised of second-hand clothing and hand-me-downs from my uncles when they were serving in the armed forces.

*   *   *   *

It was during my time of improved financial position and smarter appearance that I met my first regular girlfriend. For me it was a case of love at first sight when I met Felicity Farnley. I was out with Cyril Magwick, on our usual late afternoon stroll, me looking for compliant females and Cyril, because he had nothing better to do, accompanying me.

Felicity, who was with a friend at the time, displayed a rather haughty manner and I didn't think I would get anywhere with her, but after a brief chat up and a dose of flattery, she became more amenable and accepted my request for a date.

I hoped that Cyril might find Felicity's friend, Peggy Plumpton, sexually desirable enough to ask her out, to make a foursome for a visit to the cinema. Unfortunately at that time he found a plate of steak and kidney pudding and mash a more attractive proposition than any girl who came his way.

I later found out that Felicity and her friend were both 14 and attending grammar school. Mind you, Felicity looked and acted much older than her years and had the developed figure of a girl of 17 or eighteen.

Now that I had a regular girlfriend who enjoyed being taken out to the cinema and theatre, it was necessary for me to continue with my present fiddles and find new ones if I was to retain her interest and develop a more personal relationship. I continued my foreign stamp dealings with Mossoff, although, as I found it necessary to save more stamps for the major, my income from this source was fast diminishing. The overweighted airmail letters still provided income, but the increased charges could only be applied when correspondence contained additional documents to make it appear that the extra postage rate was justified.

The bottom had fallen out of my clothing coupon market. I'd used up my 66 coupons for the year and most of the ration of coupons of those who had been prepared to sell them to me. Those who still had coupons for sale were asking the same price as I was getting from Mrs Carlton-Smythe and she wouldn't raise her price above half a crown for a coupon.

To make matters worse, the major arranged for an auditor to check all the office accounts. Humbledick broke the news to me in a state of near panic. 'Rodney Uppersdyke is to carry out an audit of all the office records this week. Make sure your postage register balances and that all postage costs were justified. Rodney doesn't miss a thing. I remember the last audit he did, he found a deficiency of sixpence in the petty cash ledger and spent three days trying to find out what had happened to it. The longer he spent looking for it the more convinced he became that

I, or our previous office boy, had pinched it. The lad was in near tears at the thought that he might get the sack if the cash wasn't properly accounted for. What saved the day for him was finding a screwed up receipt for sixpence, for a packet of pen nibs, in his raincoat pocket. He'd forgotten to give me the receipt to enter into the petty cash ledger. Of course the major was hopping mad that his auditor had to waste so much time searching for the error and reprimanded us both for "neglect of duty" as he put it.'

'My postage register is absolutely correct and bang up to date,' I said, with an assurance I didn't feel.

'Good, but our ledgers are not the only things the major has Rodney look at. He also checks that all our contracts have been amended to show any increases that have occurred since the last audit. You'd better check all the cablegrams and letters we've received for the past year and see that all the affected contract forms have been amended.'

I set to my given task, but my mind was thinking about the missing receipt, the finding of which had satisfied the auditor that the sixpence had been a justified expenditure. Suppose, I thought, a couple of receipts, for more expensively priced items, were altered to show that the items had cost about ten per cent more? Humbledick never queried the price of anything once he'd made his entry in the petty cash book and the receipt had been filed for the next audit. The auditor wasn't interested in the price of things, only that there was a receipt to cover any expenditure, so the validity of the receipt would remain unquestioned—or so I thought.

CHAPTER 11

▼

Cyril and I were sitting in my attic bedroom, trying to think of new ways of raising money to pay for our cigarettes, visits to the cinema and eating out at Manzies Eel and Pie Shop.

'I've been giving a lot of thought lately to starting a lending library. We've belonged to that library in Herbert Road for about two years. The bloke who runs it must have made a fortune from us with all the books we've borrowed during that time.'

'But where are you going to get enough books to start a lending library?' queried Cyril, with a puzzled expression on his face.

'You're forgetting all the books I brought back from the American base at High Wycombe. The ones the club manager gave me. You've been reading them,' I replied sharply, annoyed by Cyril's lack of enthusiasm for my idea.

'Oh, *those* books—but they're not like library books; they've not got stiff covers. They're paperbacks and wouldn't last long being handled by a lot of different borrowers.'

'They'll last long enough to provide us with some money. Anyway, we'll pick our customers carefully; only lend them to adults, who know how to look after books.'

'OK, Archie, they're your books to do with what you like so how do we go about starting a library?'

Good, he's beginning to show some interest, I thought. Cyril was always sceptical when I introduced a new idea to his thinking, but he usually came around to accepting my schemes.

'Well, to start off, we'll need to catalogue all the books by author and title, and make out a card index system for booking out the books to borrowers; the same sort of system they use in the public libraries. Of course, all the books will have to be stamped with the name of our library. That'll be a good job for you. You can make up a rubber stamp with my Bulldog printing set. We could call ourselves the *C and M Library*. Better include this address, in case any of the books get lost.'

'How much would we charge for lending the books?' asked Cyril.

'We'll charge exactly the same as all the other private libraries do—tuppence a week.'

'Do you think that borrowers will pay the same for our books as they would for those being borrowed from a proper library? I know your mother isn't going to stand for people traipsing in and out of your house all day collecting and returning books,' said Cyril, with a hint of triumph in his tone.

'Oh, you of little faith, Cyril—you must trust my judgement in these matters. My plan is to take the library to the customers, show them our catalogue and let them choose their books in advance. We'll then return later with the books of their choice or, if their chosen books are not available, book them for them as soon as they are returned from the current borrower. With that sort of service, I'm sure they'll be happy to pay the normal borrowing charge.'

'Well, you do seem to have given it a lot of thought, Archie, and I suppose it's worth a go; but tell me, how do you propose to deliver all the books?'

'That'll depend on how many customers we have. If we only have a dozen or so, we can carry the books in a suitcase. If we're lucky enough to have many more customers, we'll borrow an old pram; then, if we have to deliver the books in the rain, they will be protected.'

'That sounds OK, but whatever happens, don't think I'm going to push a bloody pram around the neighbourhood all day and get silly old women asking me if they can have a look at the baby.'

'Cyril, it's a promise, *I'll* push the pram, but you can climb up the steps to the front doors with the catalogue and take the orders,' I said with finality.

*   *   *   *

Initially, our library project was moderately successful, but sadly, short-lived, principally because our customers turned out to be mainly middle-aged and elderly women, who wanted to read romantic novels, a genre of which we were in short supply. Despite employing our most persuasive 'marketing techniques' we could get few of our female customers to change their loyalties from authors like Georgette Heyer and Barbara Cartland to writers like Peter Cheyney and James Hadley Chase.

CHAPTER 12

▼

Terry Ramsbottom, one of my former fellow pupils at Fox Hill Elementary School, was waiting on the platform of Woolwich Arsenal railway station when I arrived. Like me, I thought, to save money, he is here to catch the latest workmen's train to Cannon Street. He worked for a tea importer, with offices in Plantation House on Fenchurch Street.

We had never been friends at school. He had been the most unpopular pupil in the class, mainly because he always had a huge supply of sweets, most likely bought on the 'black market' by his well-off parents, and never once offered them to any of his classmates. He was also the most disruptive of pupils and frequently gave our teacher, Mr. Holland, or 'Old Dutch', as we called him, good reason to reach for his cane in anger. On one occasion he had chased Ramsbottom around the assembly hall, lashing at his backside while we in the classroom sat silently, but deriving much pleasure from Ramsbottom's yells as 'Old Dutch' scored direct hits on his posterior. Now, because we both worked in the city and travelled on the same train each morning, we'd formed a sometimes strained, but tolerable relationship.

Ramsbottom's main topic of conversation was Charlton Athletic Football Club and despite my efforts to steer the conversation to something of more interest to me, he would speak unendingly about their current performance.

'I really fancy Charlton's chances in the FA Cup this year. They're sure to thrash Derby County. You can bet your shirt on the 'Addicks' taking the cup; it's a certainty,' pontificated Ramsbottom.

I tried to look interested and lit my first Wild Player's Weight of the morning. Ramsbottom didn't smoke. He took a large bag of boiled sweets, probably mint humbugs, from his raincoat pocket, and before continuing his ceaseless adulation of his favourite soccer team, popped a sweet into his mouth.

'Would you like to bet on the result? I'd give you good odds. What about you making a sixpenny bet that Derby beat Charlton? I'd give you odds of five to one that Charlton beat Derby, which means that if Derby beat Charlton I'd pay you two and six. Can't be fairer than that, can I?' Ramsbottom droned on.

'Frankly, Terry, I don't give a toss who wins the cup final. As I've told you on many occasions, I'm not in the least interested in football, but if it'll stop you waffling on about Charlton Athletic's chances in the cup final for the rest of this journey, I'll willingly place a bet that Derby beats Charlton,' I said with passion.

Ramsbottom beamed. 'Good, then it's settled, you bet me sixpence that Derby will beat Charlton and I'll bet a half a crown that they don't. In the unlikely event that Charlton loses, I'll pay you two and six, OK?'

'Yes, Terry, that's OK. Now, tell me, have you read any good books lately,' I added, to change the subject.

*   *   *   *

It was a much crestfallen Ramsbottom who boarded the workmen's train to Cannon Street on the following Monday morning. So disappointed was he that his beloved 'Addicks' had lost four-one to Derby County that I almost didn't have the heart to remind him that he owed me half a crown.

One thing that my surprise win taught me was that there is no such thing as a 'certainty' in life.

CHAPTER 13

▼

'Is that *another* new suit you're wearing, Terry? I don't know how you can afford to keep buying new clothes. You can't be picking up any more money than I am, and where do you get your clothing coupons? You must have used up this year's allowance in the last couple of months. Do your parents still buy your clothes?'

Ramsbottom nearly choked on his humbug. 'No, they bloody well don't! Unlike you, I don't smoke and drink, and I never spend money needlessly. You're always taking girls to the pictures—'

'Only one girl, at a time,' I interrupted. 'What about all the football matches you attend?'

'I know I go to all the Charlton home matches,' admitted Ramsbottom, 'but my uncle usually takes me and pays for my ticket.'

'But what about all those sweets you're always eating? Who pays for those?'

'My mother gets them for me. She's pretty well connected when it comes to getting all sorts of stuff off the ration and, anyway, all the money I earn is mine to spend or save, just as I please. I don't have to give my parents anything for my keep.'

Ramsbottom was beginning to sound too smug for words. 'You lucky bleeder! I've always given my mother at least two-thirds of my wages, leaving just enough for train fares. If I want any clothes I buy second-hand stuff, or get my uncles' hand-me-downs. Trouble there, though, is that I'm getting bigger than any of them. My cinema, occasional drink and fag money has to come from whatever I can make on the side.'

Ramsbottom laughed so loudly that the other passengers in the crowded compartment looked up reprovingly from their crossword puzzles. Ramsbottom lowered his voice and spoke in a conspiratorial whisper. 'You poor sod, I can see where you're going wrong. You're spending money on train fares, that's something I rarely do. I've an old out-of-date season ticket in a leather case that I just flash at the ticket collector as I pass through the gate. It always works; I've never been caught and I must have saved pounds since I started working in the City. Once, when I left the ticket in another suit, I even used an old green diary. I waited on the platform until a large number of passengers were about to pass through the gate and joined them, pushing my way through. It's easy to fool those silly old ticket-collecting farts. Most of them are as blind as bats, anyway.'

I gave a shrug of resignation. 'You might think yourself too smart to come unstuck, Terry, but you should keep it in mind that there's always a first time for everything, and one of these days you're going to get caught and end up in court.'

'Never, you can bet on it, Archie. I'd give you odds!' Ramsbottom retorted sneeringly.

Despite my warning to Ramsbottom, it wasn't long before I put his devious ticket fraud to the test. On leaving for work a few mornings later, I found that I had just enough to buy ten Player's Weights, but if I did I wouldn't have any money to pay for my rail ticket. I decided to risk it. I wasn't going to spend a whole day at Carlton-Smythe's without a smoke.

I hadn't anything that resembled a railway season ticket, so I rummaged through my mother's 'miscellaneous' drawer until I found a small notebook, which she used to write her shopping list. Luckily it had a green cover. I tore this off and cut it to the size of a season ticket. I covered this with a piece of celluloid, the remains of a model aeroplane kit, and pushed it into an old suitcase label holder, which I had found on our lodger's suitcase.

I bought my cigarettes on the way to the station—an act that made me feel that I'd 'burnt my bridges'. It was easier than I thought it would be passing through the gate in the early morning. The gate was unattended; the ticket collector had probably gone for a pee or a cup of tea.

Ramsbottom was standing on the platform sucking some sort of gobstopper. He quickly put his bag of sweets away as I approached. He grinned as I joined him. 'I see you used the season ticket ruse,' he said with a smirk. 'I saw you flourishing something, ready to show the ticket collector when you came in.'

'Yes, I was a bit skint this morning so I thought I'd give your season ticket con a whirl. I didn't have an out-of-date ticket so I used this,' I said, as I produced my mock-up season ticket for his inspection.

'Bloody hell, you've made a right bollix of that! It's a good job the ticket collector wasn't at the gate. At this time in the morning, when the ticket collector is present and there are few people travelling, it's always a bit tricky getting onto the platform. If you're going to do this regularly, you'll need to make a much better job of your false season ticket than that,' said Ramsbottom in a scornful tone.

'I know,' I said with a rueful grin, as I returned the bogus ticket to my raincoat pocket.

Arriving at Cannon Street Station that evening to return home, I waved my suitcase label wallet above my head as I surged through the gate with a large group of fellow passengers.

As my train pulled into Woolwich Arsenal, I looked out of the carriage window. Bugger it, there's a ticket collector at the gate and there don't seem to be many people getting off the train. I hung back a bit until the main group of passengers reached the exit gate and, waving my ticket above the collector's head, went through with them. I thought I had got away with it when a strong hand grabbed my raised wrist. I pulled my hand free and ran out of the station, with the ticket collector in hot pursuit. This ticket collector was quite young and a fast runner, and he was right behind me as I raced along the pavement, dodging pedestrians as I ran. As I turned a corner I was stopped by the sudden presence of two very large ladies walking towards me. Before I could dodge around them my pursuer caught me by the coat collar and pulled me to a halt. He was a man of medium build, probably in his late thirties, but by the way he grasped my collar, I knew he was strong. I felt that I could have broken free from his grasp and outrun him after a few hundred yards, but I didn't; after all, he was in the right. It was a 'fair cop', and if I did resist him one of us could get hurt so, shame-facedly, I allowed him to escort me back to the station. Still grasping me by the collar he knocked on the stationmaster's office door.

'Come in,' a strong male voice invited.

The ticket collector kept his hold on my collar and we entered the office like Siamese twins and stood in front of the stationmaster's desk.

'What's the problem, Hodges?' the stationmaster asked.

Hodges gave the stationmaster my bogus season ticket and related his version of what had happened, making it sound like he'd caught a dangerous desperado single-handedly. The stationmaster listened to the story with a bored and disinterested look on his face. He's heard all this stuff before from this bloke, I thought.

'OK, Hodges, get back to your gate. I'll deal with this.'

Hodges reluctantly let go of my collar and shuffled out of the office. His expression showed that he was disappointed that his boss had not congratulated him. The stationmaster looked me over with a hint of merriment in his eyes. 'You've been a naughty young man, haven't you? You'd better explain yourself,' he said, almost light-heartedly.

I put on my most contrite expression. 'Yes, sir, I'm afraid I have. I sincerely apologise for my bad behaviour and promise that I'll never do anything like that again. The fact is I lost my return ticket and hadn't any money to buy another ticket. All the other staff had left the office before me, so I couldn't borrow money for my fare. I couldn't think of any other way to get enough money to buy a ticket so I made this up in the office.'

The stationmaster looked at me steadily for about ten seconds then almost smiled. I bet he's thinking about what he got up to in his youth, I thought.

'What you've committed is a very serious offence and could have landed you in a magistrates' court. However, in view of the circumstances, I shall not prosecute you on this occasion, but if you are ever caught at my station again without a ticket you'll be for the high jump, sonny. Now just write your full name and address on this paper. I need those details so that we can send you a bill for the journey you made from Cannon Street to this station.'

I hurriedly complied, not even considering giving a false name and address.

'Thank you, sir—I'll never try to travel without a ticket again,' I said obsequiously, and meant it.

CHAPTER 14

▼

Humbledick was out for a late lunch. I had eaten my beef dripping sandwiches and two of my mother's rock cakes, washed down with a bottle of ginger beer, and was working on the *Daily Mirror* crossword. The major had visited the office late that morning and entertained one of our South American principals. The major had sent me out to buy his specially ordered and prepared sandwiches from a Fenchurch Street delicatessen. When I took the sandwiches to his office I noticed an open box of 50 Abdullah cigarettes, a bottle of Johnny Walker Black Label whisky and two cut glass whisky glasses on the major's desk. Nothing but the best for our principals, I thought.

'Here, put the sandwiches on these plates, Cholmondeley,' ordered the major, indicating two paper plates on his desk.

I placed the greaseproof paper wrapped sandwiches on the plates and turned to leave his office.

'Cholmondeley!' boomed the major. 'Haven't you forgotten something? What about my change? I gave you two half-crowns for four bob's worth of sandwiches, so I should have a shilling change.'

'Oh yes, of course, sir,' I said, as I sheepishly withdrew a shilling from my jacket pocket and handed it to him. 'I'm sorry, sir, it slipped my mind.'

As I walked out of the office, I heard the major say to his South American guest: 'He's a bright lad, but you have to watch him. He's as artful as a wagon load of monkeys.'

A half an hour later the major and his guest had left his office to attend a meeting with some big shot from Houlder Brothers shipping company, and it was unlikely that they would return to the office. This got me thinking about the box of cigarettes and bottle of whisky. Unnecessarily furtively, I entered the major's office. Apart from three ancient wicker baskets, a telephone, a silver pen rack and a leather-bound blotter, the major's desk was empty. The paper plates and sandwich wrapping paper were in the wastepaper basket at the side of his desk. He had put the goodies away, most likely in his desk, because apart from two easy chairs and a small occasional table, the only other furniture in the office was an open bookcase. I tried the desk drawers, but they were all locked. I looked in the obvious place for his keys—hanging on a hook under the desk. I opened the largest bottom drawer first. Bingo, the drawer contained the opened bottle of Johnny Walker, two other unopened bottles of whisky and several boxes of different cigarettes. I took five or six cigarettes from an opened box of Players and shuffled the remainder around to make the gap in the top row less noticeable. I took a generous swig from the whisky bottle, making a mental note to replace what I had taken with tap water at the first opportunity.

Returning to the general office, I lit one of my pilfered cigarettes and put my feet up on my desk, where they would remain until I heard the unmistakable plodding gait of Humbledick as he walked up the corridor to our office.

When Humbledick entered the office, I was reading the day's cablegrams.

'The price of coffee has gone up again in Brazil,' I said to him, as though I was genuinely concerned.

'That's quite extraordinary, when you consider how much coffee they have in Brazil,' replied Humbledick, in an equally concerned tone of voice.

'Yes,' I said, unable to resist it, 'they've got an *awful lot* of coffee in Brazil.'

CHAPTER 15

▼

I was sitting in my mother's unused dining room with Johnny Sheldrake, one of my better-educated friends. He was a year or two older than me, had gone to a grammar school, worked in Martins Bank and could play chess well enough to beat most of the members of The Gambit Club. Johnny had expensive tastes; he smoked Kensitas or Senior Service cigarettes, drank brandy and actually liked it, always sat in the circle seats at the cinema and without fail caught a bus rather than walk the relatively short distance to his home.

We were discussing new ways and means of making some easy money.

'Well, what do you think of my rodent exterminator, Archie?' asked Johnny.

'Explain it to me again, Johnny. There seems to be a flaw in your scheme. For a start, I can't imagine people paying five bob for a small block of wood and a little mallet, and then there's your guarantee that if the exterminator doesn't work they'll get their money refunded.'

'Nothing wrong with the guarantee, it'll give them confidence in purchasing our little gizmo (Johnny loved using newly coined words). The instructions for using the device are simple enough: *Place offending rodent on block of wood and strike head of rodent repeatedly with mallet until rodent is dead or insensible then, to ensure its demise, immerse rodent in a bucket of water.'*

I wasn't convinced. 'Don't you think that people will see it as a big con when they receive your blocks of wood and mallets in the post? They'll have to catch the rodents before they place them on their block, and that's not so easy.'

'So what! We're not saying anything about how they should catch the rodents, but simply providing them with a humane means for the destruction of the rodents, without the need for them to spread virulent substances about their property, which could well harm young children and domestic animals. Nothing illegal about that, and we only refund their money if they fail to *kill* the rodent with the wooden mallet.'

'OK, Johnny, you've had your little joke, but this was supposed to be a serious discussion about making money—honestly. Well, almost honestly.'

Johnny took a sip of his 'cooking brandy' and lit a cigarette, a Kensita, but didn't offer me one of his 'four for your friends'. I'll remember that, I thought, when he's on the scrounge for a cigarette, any sort of cigarette.

'All right, let's hear what you propose,' asked Johnny, drawing deeply on his cigarette.'

'Well, sit back and listen to my scheme. Tell me, apart from sex, what do young people like to do, or would like to do, if they had the money to do it?'

Johnny looked puzzled and scratched his head, disarraying his lank and prematurely thinning, mousy coloured hair. 'Travel, I suppose, buy the latest fashions in clothing, that's if they can get hold of the necessary clothing coupons, eat out at expensive restaurants—'

'You're getting warm, Johnny,' I interrupted, 'but what else?'

'Oh, yes, I suppose some of them would like to gamble and drink.'

'Exactly, and that's what we are going to give them the opportunity to do, with little expense to them and, perhaps, a not too little profit for us. I suggest we start a gambling club.'

Johnny looked dumbfounded. 'Where the blazes are you going to hire the premises to do that?'

'Right here, in this very room; we've got all the furniture we need—a table, six chairs and a sideboard, and there's the built-in cupboard.'

'Will your mother and stepfather, Eddie, allow you to do that? Have people coming in at all hours and leaving late at night—I should think not.'

'The club will only be open from seven to nine on about four nights a week. I shall tell my mother and Eddie that we have formed a drama group and the people who come here are rehearsing a play to be put on at the Young Conservatives' Club.'

Johnny began to show some interest. 'OK, so you've got your club premises, but what about all the equipment you'd need?'

'I've got stacks of playing cards, dice for playing craps, three boxes of real poker chips, a small roulette wheel, a Crown and Anchor board complete with dice, and some poker dice. What else does one need?'

Johnny looked impressed. 'Where did you get all that stuff from?'

'I got them from the American base at High Wycombe, where I was working, when it was closed down. The top sergeant who managed the Aero Club said I could take anything I wanted from the club's games' room and the club library, so I helped myself to everything of use, and my mother and I had it all carted to this address by a removals firm when we returned from High Wycombe. You must remember those paperback books—I used them to start a mobile library.'

'Yes, I remember you telling me that you and Cyril Magwick had started a library, but as I recall, it didn't last long, did it?'

'No, not very long, but the idea was sound; we just had problems satisfying all the literary tastes of our borrowers.'

'So far, so good, but what games are we going to provide and who will act as croupiers and dealers?'

Johnny was starting to get technical, as he always did when we were planning any new project.

'Who else, but you and me,' I testily replied. 'You are a good poker player, so you can run a game using that occasional table. Or, if you'd rather, you can take charge of the Crown and Anchor board. I'll look after the roulette wheel, which can go on the dining table and I've got an old miniature snooker table we could use for playing craps on.'

'Craps! How vulgar. What are they?'

'Really, I am surprised that you've never heard of craps. It's a dice game they play in America. The guys at the base showed me how to play. It'll be a winner for us,' I enthused.

'What about drinks?' asked Johnny. 'They're always available at gambling clubs.'

'We could water down whisky. Those who haven't tasted it before wouldn't know the difference. We could also use ginger wine; it's quite strong and could be watered down. There's also shandy; a quart bottle of ale mixed with a similar quantity of lemonade would provide about 16 drinks and furnish us with a nice profit.'

'Well, I've got to hand it to you, Archie, you've certainly thought of most things, but who'll serve the drinks?'

'The hostess for the club will be none other than my smashing new girlfriend, Felicity. She's a charmer and a real Sarah Bernhardt character, who'll know how to act and dress for the part. You've met her— don't you agree with my choice?'

Johnny did, and I knew why as he had a crush on her himself and would need watching.

✳   ✳   ✳   ✳

Our venture into running The Dark Town gaming club, as Johnny, an ardent fan of Phil Harris, insisted on it being called, lasted about two weeks. We had managed to attract about a dozen young guys and gals to join the club. They were given a membership card, printed with my Bulldog printing set, for their sixpence membership fee, and their first drink was on the house.

Initially, they were all keen to try their luck with our various games. Roulette proved to be the favourite, but their interest soon waned when they lost the little money they had been prepared to gamble. The shandy sold well to the girls, but the watered down whisky, sherry and ginger wine was not very well received by some of the more experienced drinkers. As a result, there were several nasty stains to be removed from the dining room carpet.

My mother and Eddie never entered the room, but Eddie, a staunch socialist, complained to me in the morning that he couldn't hear the radio because of all the noise made by the Young Conservative 'play actors' and suggested, none too politely, that we rehearse our play somewhere else, preferably at the Conservative Club

When the operation was closed down, some of the members voiced the opinion that their membership fees should be refunded. Johnny solved the problem to our advantage by inviting them to play a one-hand game of poker, using the jokers and deuces as wild cards. If he lost they'd get their money back. If he won they could 'bloody well belt up!'

Johnny won, but there were mutterings among the club members that 'he'd cheated by dropping the wildies down between his knees'.

CHAPTER 16

▼

Business was slack and during such rare occasions, Humbledick would fill our time by relating incidents from his past life and stories about former members of staff. Sometimes his stories were of a very personal nature. On one such occasion he brought up the subject of his wife's inability to become pregnant.

'We've been trying for a baby ever since we were married four years ago. I thought at first it might be because I am 15 years older than my wife, but I've been told that doesn't make any difference—'

'That's right, for sure,' I interrupted. 'My grandfather was 20 years older than my grandmother and they had 11 kids. She even had twins when she was forty-eight!'

Humbledick raised his eyebrows and continued, 'We've had sex four or five times a week for months, without any success; then we went a month without having it at all and still had no luck. We've tried all the various positions, but nothing seems to work.'

I put on a sympathetic look and nodded sagely. 'It must be very disappointing for you and your wife. Have you thought about adopting a child? There must be thousands of war orphans who need mothers and fathers?'

Humbledick frowned and looked ill at ease. 'That would be the very last resort for Dorothy as she desperately wants a child of her own and, anyway, you never know what you are getting when you adopt from an orphanage, especially shortly after a war.'

An opportunity to change the subject, I thought. 'What did you do in the war, Mr Humbledick? You don't look like a soldier.'

Humbledick reddened slightly and hesitated for a few seconds before he answered. 'I was found medically unfit for military service so I volunteered to be a special constable. They were glad to get me. There was a shortage of policemen when they needed them most. War or no war, crimes were still being committed and there was also the risk of sabotage and enemy agents getting into the country. A lot of time was spent checking the identity of the thousands of foreign soldiers and refugees who came to this country. Good thing we had identity cards. It made the job a lot easier.'

'Yes, I'm sure it did,' I said, beginning to become bored with Humbledick's account of his service as a special constable. 'I still have my identity card. I suppose we might have to hand them in some time.'

Before Humbledick could answer, the telephone rang. Saved by the bell, I thought. Humbledick snatched up the phone. 'Royal 6039, Humbledick speaking,' he announced.

It must have been a call from the major because Humbledick stood up at his desk and almost came to attention.

'Yes, sir, I'll see to that straight away. As you suggest—a little job for Cholmondeley.'

Humbledick replaced the phone and turned to me. 'The major wants to have his wicker baskets replaced before he comes to the office next week. He suggests that you go to that stationers at the end of Fenchurch Street and buy three new ones. He also wants you to neatly print three cards for attachment to the baskets: "in", "out" and "pending". You can go after the lunch break. I'll give you 30 shillings, which should be more than enough to buy them.'

'OK, Mr Humbledick, I'll go in my lunch break,' I volunteered, remembering that I had some stamps to take to Mossoff's shop. 'It'll save a bit of time.'

'Very well, Archie,' agreed Humbledick, reaching for his petty cash tin and withdrawing two banknotes, a pound note and a ten-shilling note. 'Make sure you get the right change and don't forget the sales slip. I'll need it to support my entry in the cashbook. Mr. Uppersdyke is so particular about such things and requires a receipt for every penny spent.'

'Surely not for postage stamps because they are receipts in themselves, aren't they?' I asked.

'No, of course not,' replied Humbledick, with a short laugh. 'Since you are going in your own time, you can go to lunch early. Pop off now if you like.'

I needed no second bidding. I hastily donned my raincoat and was out of the office and running down the corridor like Sydney Wooderson in training for the 5,000 yards.

I called into Mossoff's and presented the few stamps that I had saved during the past month. Mossoff gave them a cursory glance and, without a word, passed me a two-shilling piece. Not much, but it would pay for a one and nine penny cinema ticket, a tuppenny block of ice cream and a bus ride home.

'I would like to see your range of wicker baskets. The sort you use for holding papers,' I asked in a business-like tone of voice.

The shop assistant, a middle-aged woman, smiled and opened a display cabinet behind the counter and produced a wicker basket. 'This is the only type we stock,' she said, placing it on the counter.

I picked it up and went through the motions as though I was examining its woven workmanship. 'Yes, this should be suitable for what I want. I'd like three, please. How much are they?'

'These have been reduced in price and are now only three and sixpence each.'

I handed her the pound note and she gave me nine and sixpence change. The woman made a brown paper parcel of the three trays and made out a sales slip.

I was pleased to note that she used one of those new biro pens, a black one. I still had several that I had found in the Aero Club, and I had a black biro in my pocket.

Entering the ABC restaurant, I ordered a cup of tea and two Chelsea buns, and took them to a corner table. I examined the sales slip, which read: *Three wicker filing baskets at 3/6p each, total 10/6p.* The threes shouldn't be too difficult to alter to fives, and the shop assistant had said that the baskets had been reduced in price so 5/6p each shouldn't be considered too much to pay for them. I carefully altered the threes to fives, and the total cost of 10/6p into 16/6p. Not bad, a clear profit of six shillings, which I deducted from the 19/6p change the shop assistant had given me, and placed in an inside pocket of my jacket.

I stayed in the restaurant for about half an hour drinking my tea, eating my Chelsea buns and smoking a cigarette while planning what I would do with my unexpected windfall.

Returning to the office, I unwrapped the baskets and placed them on the corner of Humbledick's desk.

'Yes, they look all right,' said Humbledick. 'Change and sales slip, please.'

I placed the change and the sales slip on the desk. 'Shall I make out the cards for fixing to the baskets?' I asked, not to please, but to divert Humbledick's gaze from the sales slip.

'Yes, as soon as you like. There's a stencil set in the stationary cupboard. Use that, it'll make a better job of it than your printing.'

I collected the stencil set and white cardboard from the cupboard and took them to my desk, watching Humbledick out of the corner of my eye as he stared fixedly at the sales slip. Surely he hadn't seen the alterations? He turned the slip over and looked at the back for a few seconds, then, obviously in an attempt to do so covertly, slipped the sales slip into his trouser pocket. 'I'm just popping out for a few minutes to get some pipe tobacco,' he said as he walked to the clothes stand to put on his jacket.

Without another word, Humbledick, his face averted, but not so that I couldn't see his grave expression, walked out of the office. That's it then, the game's up. The sly old bugger has spotted the alterations. I underestimated him; I should have remembered that he'd had police training with the 'specials'. Nothing for it, I thought, as I entered the major's office, opened his bottom drawer, took out his now well-diluted bottle of whisky, opened it and took a generous swallow. I then returned the bottle to the drawer and helped myself to three or four cigarettes from the box of Abdullahs. Returning to the general office, I lit one of the cigarettes, put my feet up on the desk and waited, with growing dread, for the return of Humbledick.

He wasn't long; I'd barely finished the cigarette before he returned. He strode into the office without giving me a look or taking off his jacket. He sniffed the air as if there was a bad smell in the office, and sat down at his desk, picked up the phone and dialled a number. Bloody hell, he's smelled the Turkish fag, I thought. It gets worse.

'Hello, sir, I'm sorry to bother you at home, but I thought you ought to be told straight away. I'm afraid Cholmondeley has been guilty of a very serious act of larceny. He has falsified a sales slip and embezzled six shillings...'

Crikey, is he talking about *me*? You'd think I'd stolen the crown jewels, the way he is laying it on.

Humbledick went on…'Do you wish me to take any disciplinary action in the matter? Shall I dismiss him?' Humbledick stopped talking and listened intently. 'Very well, sir, if that is your decision. Oh, so you're not coming in until Friday next week? Very well, sir, I'll do nothing about it until I see you next Friday. Goodbye, sir.'

Humbledick replaced the receiver and turned to me. 'How on earth did you think you could get away with a trick like that?'

I put on a shame-faced expression, but said nothing. As the major had obviously told Humbledick that he would deal with the matter himself when he came to the office next Friday, I had a 'stay of execution' and thought it best not to say anything until I appeared before the major. My grandfather had once told me, 'Whenever you find yourself in a hole, stop digging!'

It was Friday afternoon, so I kept my head down and concentrated on amending shipowners' contract price lists. The time to pack up for the weekend couldn't come soon enough. As soon as it did I started to put things away.

Humbledick didn't look at me when he handed me my wage packet. 'You can go now. I'll finish putting everything away.'

While I was putting my coat on he went into the major's office. Seconds later I heard a noise that had become familiar to me, the slight metallic sound of a key being lifted off a metal hook. Removing the major's key—he really has got me. The major's bound to sack me when he hears that I've been looting his bottom drawer.

I left the office and slowly walked to London Bridge station, thinking all the time of how I was going to talk my way out of getting sacked. Still, I had a week to come up with something and with the stamp money and my 'embezzled' six shillings I had eight bob, more than enough to console me over the weekend. I'd take Felicity to the cinema, probably buy her a small box of chocs or take her to a café for fish and chips when we left the cinema. Afterwards, we could just see what came up. Things could be a lot worse.

I enjoyed a weekend of sheer indulgence with Felicity. We went to the cinema to see *Crossfire,* a rattling good film, starring three of my favourite film star Roberts: Mitchum, Ryan and Young. I bought large ice cream tubs in the cinema and we finished off Felicity's box of chocolates on the way home, via the scenic route—Oxleas Wood and Eltham Common. There I enjoyed a brief, but nonetheless, most satisfactory dalliance with Felicity.

Monday morning came early. I had slept little and arose before my alarm went off, but my near sleepless night had not been wasted; I had planned a strategy. I would attempt to redeem myself with a display of unrelenting industry.

I arrived at the office at seven-thirty. I knew that Humbledick wouldn't appear much before nine o'clock, allowing plenty of time for me to do what I had to do. I tidied the office, completed the labels and fixed them neatly to the major's new baskets and placed them on his desk. I put the old baskets in the bottom of the stationary cupboard; we might find a use for them later. I checked the revised price lists and amended the appropriate contract forms.

By the time Humbledick arrived in the office, to be greeted by me with a cheery, 'Good morning, Mr Humbledick, I hope you had a pleasant weekend', I had virtually carried out a normal day's work.

Humbledick mumbled, 'Good morning', without looking at me as he took off his coat. Sitting at his desk he viewed his overflowing in-tray of amended contracts and cablegrams for him to check. 'You

have been busy. Did you come back to the office and work all night?'
he asked, without a trace of humour in his tone.

'No, I got in very early and managed to catch up with all the pending correspondence and amendments,' I replied.

I could see Humbledick was favourably impressed by the amount of
work I had done before he had arrived in the office, but he said nothing and, to my relief, never mentioned anything more about my
'embezzlement'.

I kept up a non-stop work activity throughout the day, not even taking time out to light a cigarette and relax for a minute or two. I
replaced worn and tatty file covers, printed new contents labels for the
filing cabinets and contract forms drawers and, when Humbledick was
out to lunch, cleaned the inside surfaces and frames of the office windows.

When Humbledick returned he stood in the doorway and gave a
clearly audible, 'Hmm', before taking off his coat and sitting at his
desk. Suddenly, turning to me, he said: 'Aren't you going out today?'

'No, I want to clear all these amendments before home time.'

Humbledick smiled with his eyes and started to wade through the
fresh pile of contracts, letters and cablegrams I had left in his tray.

I followed the same routine on Tuesday and Wednesday, but it was
getting difficult to find jobs to keep me occupied. On Thursday I
decided to go out for a late lunch and sat for about an hour drinking
tea and smoking in the ABC restaurant, trying to formulate a plan of
defence for when I was faced with what, I anticipated, would be a
major onslaught in the morning.

Sitting at the next table were two typical, pinstriped city gents, who
were talking rather loudly. One almost shouted: 'Have you heard the
latest, Ralph? That socialist cretin, Hugh Dalton, intends to put up the
price of 20 cigarettes from two and fourpence to three and fourpence

in today's budget. Of course, it's only a rumour, but I did hear it from a very reliable source.'

'That's a whole shilling on a packet of Players, Arnold,' his companion replied. 'The man must be stark raving mad to do a thing like that. The British public won't stand for it. It would never have happened under Churchill's premiership.'

'I don't think they'll have much choice in the matter, Ralph. It's obvious what the Labour Party are up to—they want the extra revenue to help fund their crackpot scheme to create a National Health Service.'

'What you're saying explains why I couldn't buy any cigarettes anywhere this morning. The crafty tobacconists must be keeping them under the counter until tomorrow to…'

I switched off from listening to their depressing conversation and went back to planning my defence, but the thought of having to pay about tenpence more, I guessed, for a packet of 20 of the cheaper brands of cigarettes that I usually smoked, only added to my gloom.

*   *   *   *

I took special pains over my appearance before I set off to work on Friday morning. I bathed, shaved, cut and cleaned my nails, brushed and pressed my suit, put on a freshly laundered shirt and neatly knotted my most sober necktie. I had been to the barbers on my way home the previous evening and before I went to bed I washed my hair. Looking at myself in my wardrobe mirror I felt that I looked smart enough to face the major's critical eye.

Ramsbottom was on the platform when I arrived at the station.

'Bloody hell!' exclaimed Ramsbottom. 'Are you off to a wedding or something? You look dressed to kill. Have you got a new bird you're trying to impress?'

'No, nothing like that, I have an important interview with my boss. He wants to discuss my progress with a view to considering me for a different position,' I said, without a trace of a smile on my face.

Ramsbottom seemed suitably impressed and made no further mention of my appearance during our journey to Cannon Street. His parting shot, as we separated in Fenchurch Street, was very predictable.

'How do you fancy Charlton's chances tomorrow?'

'I expect them to get their usual thrashing from some second-rate northern team,' I shouted back with a laugh.

As I turned to walk in the direction of Lloyds Avenue, an unshaven and ashen-faced man of about 30 stepped out of a shop doorway. He was wearing a torn and stained army battledress and an equally stained khaki shirt. His long lank hair was tangled and stood out in profusion from under a heavily grease-stained cloth cap. He limped towards me in what had once been white plimsolls, but they were now grey with dirt and holed at the toes. He stretched out his grubby right hand towards me. It was missing two fingers and was hideously scarred. "Ave yer got tuppence for a cuppa tea, guv?' he whined beseechingly, in a strong cockney accent.

Guv—me? I must have looked perplexed or perhaps he thought me deaf.

'Please, guv, I ain't 'ad a drink o' tea for days.'

The penny dropped. He was calling me 'guv' because I was smartly dressed and looked much older than seventeen. I knew exactly what I had in my pocket—two sixpenny pieces, enough to buy me ten Player's Weights, a cup of tea and a buttered roll. However, this poor bleeder was an ex-soldier, down on his luck, who looked as though he'd been horribly wounded in the war. I reached into my pocket and withdrew one of the sixpences. No, that wasn't enough. My hand returned to my pocket and withdrew both coins. This man was going to have a meal today. I passed them to him and he took them from me with his half a hand and clutched them tightly. 'Gawd bless yer, guv, yor a toff,' he said, the whine gone from his voice, as he saluted me with his still clutched crippled hand.

'Good luck, mate,' I replied, with a mock salute, and continued on my way to the office. Perhaps giving that poor sod the last of my 'embezzled' cash was a good omen; things might not go so bad for me at my interview with the major, but I knew that was probably a pipe dream.

It was a little after ten o'clock when the major arrived at the office. Humbledick and I arose from our desks and gave him our customary greeting: 'Good morning, sir.'

He didn't look at me, but to Humbledick he almost shouted: 'My office in five minutes, Humbledick.'

I returned to my work.

Exactly five minutes later, Humbledick stood up from his desk carrying a small sheaf of papers, the sales slip almost certainly among them, in his hand and knocked on the major's door.

'Come in!' bawled the major.

Humbledick entered the office and quietly closed the door behind him. I strained my ears, but could catch little of what was said. It must have been a good half an hour before Humbledick opened the major's door and called me in. I stood in front of the major's desk and looked fixedly at a picture of a Shaw Saville Line ship just above the major's head. I prayed that the major had had a good breakfast on the train from Wiltshire and that nothing, so far that morning, had caused him any irritation.

'Stay and be seated, Humbledick,' ordered the major in a voice that told me he was not in the best of moods.

The major looked at me searchingly, as if he hadn't seen me before. 'I presume you know why you are in front of me this morning, Cholmondeley?'

'Yes, sir,' I immediately replied, 'Mr Humbledick advised me.'

'Well, I shall first deal with the lesser charge against you. Humbledick has reported to me that you have been stealing my Abdullah cigarettes and have had the temerity to smoke them in the office. He says that when he entered the office last Friday he distinctly smelled the aroma of one of my cigarettes. What have you to say in your defence?'

'Only this, sir,' I replied, as I pulled a crumpled Abdullah cigarette packet from my pocket and laid it on his desk. I had rescued the packet from a wastepaper bin in the saloon bar of a local pub. The packet now contained two of the major's Abdullah cigarettes.

'What is this piece of rubbish you have put on my desk?' the major asked, almost exploding.

'It is an almost empty packet of Abdullah cigarettes. I believe there are two cigarettes left in it. I took to trying out the brand after a visiting ship chandler smoked one in your office. It was the aroma of one of these cigarettes that Mr Humbledick smelled when he came into the office,' I said, trying not to sound too smug.

The major glared at Humbledick, who was sitting in the corner of the room behind me.

'Very well, I find *that* charge unproved.' The major glanced at the notes in front of him. 'Now, I shall deal with a much graver offence. Did you or did you not alter the figures on this sales receipt to enable you to embezzle the sum of six shillings?'

'Yes, sir, I did and I humbly seek your forgiveness for my most regrettable act of dishonesty.'

The major seemed taken aback by my ready and forthright admission, and before he could respond I took a deep breath and launched into my rehearsed defence plea.

'The fact is, sir, I have to help support my widowed mother on the very lowly wage I am paid by you. I sometimes supplement my earnings by doing odd jobs for relatives and neighbours, but of late, little work has come my way. To make matters even worse, my dear mother lost her purse last weekend so, because of the dire straits in which she found herself, with insufficient money to pay our rent, household expenses and my train fares to work, when the opportunity to make a few shillings by falsifying a sales slip occurred, I was sorely tempted; but I assure you that it is the first time I have ever carried out such a felonious deed and swear that I shall never do so again. I know it won't excuse my action, but I should like to add that the baskets had been reduced in price and were in fact worth two shillings more than their stated price. So, what I did was to merely extract the amount by which they had been reduced.'

'My word, Cholmondeley, you do put up a good defence for your wrongdoing, I'll give you that. Nevertheless, it was a wrongdoing and utterly criminal, and you could have ended up in court if I had wished to have you prosecuted. However, from what you have said, and taking account what Mr Humbledick has told me about how hard you have been working to atone for your act, on this occasion I shall admonish you; but I warn you that should anything like this occur again you will be dismissed instantly. Do I make myself clear, Cholmondeley?'

'Perfectly, sir,' I said, resisting a smile that was beginning to curl my lips. 'Will that be all, sir?'

'No, hold your horses, Cholmondeley, I haven't finished with you yet.' The major leaned forward over his desk, looked up at me and smiled thinly. 'Having given consideration to all the factors in this case and bearing in mind your mother's financial circumstances, I have decided to increase your wages by five shillings a week, starting from next pay day. With regard to the problem you have in making ends meet, I would suggest that you give some thought about smoking a more affordable brand of cigarettes. Now get back in the general office and start earning your increase in wages.'

'Thank you, sir; I can assure you I shall not be smoking any more Abdullah cigarettes. As a matter of fact, after yesterday's budget increase in the price of cigarettes, I very much doubt that I'll be able to afford to smoke even the cheapest brand of cigarettes,' I said, with tongue in cheek as I left his office.

*   *   *   *

'How did you get on at the interview with your boss,' asked Ramsbottom, as he joined me on the platform next morning.

'Oh *that*, smashing, couldn't have been better. My boss said that I was a credit to the firm and that he would be considering me for promotion in the near future, and to ensure that I wouldn't leave the firm for a better paid job before that occurred, he would give me a rise of ten shillings a week,' I lied without compunction.

'You lucky sod!' exclaimed Ramsbottom. 'If you fell into a sewage pit you'd come up smelling of roses.'

CHAPTER 17

▼

Since I had received my unexpected pay rise I had been neglecting Felicity and she wasn't backward in letting me know. 'My father says the only time we see you is when you're short of money, which is every day except Friday. You always have an excuse for not coming over to our place on Fridays. Every other night of the week you seem glad enough to be there, playing cards, teaching me card tricks, drinking my mother's 'surplus to requirements' milk, bantering with my father and—'

'You're being unfair,' I interrupted.

But Felicity wasn't to be denied her say. 'When you *do* take me out it's only to some local cinema on a Sunday afternoon to see old films, and always in the cheapest seats. On top of that you expect me to walk home, via your so-called "scenic route", when you always find a secluded spot to try to have your evil way with me.'

I put on a hurt look. 'Darling, you are being *very* unfair. I only have Fridays to go out with some of my friends. They do the same on pay-days. Anyway, I don't have much money to spend on anything or any-body. You know that I give most of my wages to my mother to help pay for the housekeeping and I have train fares to pay for as well. As for my romantic advances, I thought you enjoyed them.'

'I do, Archie, I really do, but sometimes you forget how far we agreed to go with our lovemaking, and that spoils it for me if you try to go further. With regards to your mother, I'm well aware that you are a good son to her and help her in every way you can, but you're always telling me about your moneymaking fiddles, so I naturally expect that you have sufficient cash to take me out to places other than the local bug-ridden cinemas. I like to go up town with my Uncle Vincent to the West End theatres and cinemas and eat out in proper restaurants, instead of those awful mobile coffee stalls you want to go to when we leave the cinema. So, please, can't we go somewhere different for a change? Remember, it is my birthday this coming Sunday.'

I put on my best smile and took Felicity into my arms.

'Yes, I know, darling, you'll be 16 on the sixteenth, which is a lovely age for a girl; a time when she has reached the full bloom of her youth and is most desirable.'

Felicity pulled away from me and laughed. 'You can't fool me with your romantic twaddle and I know what you're getting at—it's legal for girls to have sexual intercourse when they are sixteen. Well, that might be so for others, but *this* girl is going to be a virgin when she marries.'

I deemed it wise to change the subject. 'I wasn't going to mention it until Thursday evening, but since you have been complaining about my lack of taking you out anywhere decent, I'll let you into my little secret. I'll not be going out with any of the lads this Friday. I shall be taking you out on the town to celebrate your birthday. How does that suit you?'

Felicity smiled up at me and took my hands in hers.

'Now that's more like it, big boy. Where are you taking me?'

'You'll find out on the evening. Just be ready with your big girl's clothes on at seven o'clock on Friday evening, when I call for you. I promise to give you a night to remember.'

Felicity gave a girlish giggle. 'Ooh, an unforgettable evening out with Archie Cholmondeley, I can hardly believe it. I'll be all dolled up in my glad rags for seven. Don't you be late.'

'I'll be there with bells on, trust me.'

*   *   *   *

'Archie, if you had to take me to a pub, you could have picked a better one than this! *The Pig and Whistle*! The name says everything about the place. Why did we have to come to North Woolwich anyway when there are much better pubs south of the river? We could have gone to The Shakespeare Hotel; it's much grander, more like a night club, and they have a jazz group playing there on Fridays and Saturdays.'

'How come you know so much about Woolwich pubs? You're still at school and shouldn't be going into pubs.'

'My Uncle Vincent tells me all about them. He's been in them all. Anyway, you're not 18 until January, so what are you doing in them?'

'I've been going into pubs with my mother and relatives since I was 14 and nobody has ever questioned me about my age. Mind you, I didn't get much beer bought for me; it was usually a glass of ginger beer and an *arrowroot* biscuit. The reason I brought you over here was to start the evening with what I thought would be a romantic touch—a cruise across the Thames on the Woolwich Ferry; but that wasn't the only reason. I did think that you'd rather go somewhere where you wouldn't be recognised. You see, I do consider your reputation. Now finish that drink before it evaporates and I'll get you another gin and lime,' I said, before downing my pint of mild and bitter.

Suddenly, conversation became difficult. Someone had fed money into one of those newfangled jukeboxes in the corner immediately behind us. The Al Saxon Band were belting out 'I'm Always Chasing Rainbows'; isn't that the truth, I thought. We moved along the quieter end of the bar and I ordered more drinks. 'A double gin and lime for my missus and a pint of mild and bitter, please,' I said, as I made a show of dropping a pound note on the bar in front of the barman.

'She ain't your missus, matey,' came a gruff voice from behind me.

I turned to face a tough looking, burly man in his late thirties. He had the florid face of a hardened drinker and had missed shaving for about a week. He held a pint glass of beer in his left hand, which was shaking and slopping beer over his shoes.

'What did you say?' I asked, stalling for time to think of a stronger response.

'You 'eard, matey, she ain't your missus. She's just a tart you've picked up on the street.' The man leaned forwards, exuding his foul breath into my face.

Felicity, who had been standing away from the bar, moved nearer to me. The man swayed towards her. 'Ain't that right, sweetheart? He ain't your old man. You're just a bit of crumpet he's picked up, ain't you?'

Felicity laughed in his face, visibly wincing as she smelled his breath. 'Don't be absurd, you silly man. Of course he is my husband. As a matter of fact, we are out tonight to celebrate our wedding anniversary.'

'What's it to you, anyway?' I interposed, with an edge to my tone. 'Why don't you sit down, before you fall down?'

The man straightened himself up with an effort and looked ugly. 'Are you looking for trouble, sonny? If you are, you've just found it!'

Al Saxon's band was now playing 'When you were Sweet Sixteen', the jukebox set at an even higher volume.

'Sweet 16, that's about right; your bird's not much older than that. She's just a little tart you've picked up for quick shag outside the pub after you've got her pissed.'

Felicity looked at me appealingly. I knew I had to do something or lose face in her eyes.

'Why don't you bugger off and leave us alone,' I said, with as much menace as I could project into my voice.

The man looked surprised, then very angry, as he raised his right arm as if to strike me. I knew that, although the man was drunk, or very nearly so, I would be no match against him in a fistfight. He had the confidence of one who knew he was stronger and more experienced in brawling. There was only one thing I could think of to do. Very calmly and without drawing attention from the nearby customers, I deliberately poured the entire contents of my newly filled beer glass over the front of his trousers; then, above the sound of the Benny Goodman's rendition of 'Don't be that Way', shouted: 'You dirty sod, you've pissed all over the floor!'

The man dropped his glass, which shattered on the floor, and he stood briefly rooted to the spot as the beer dripped from his saturated trousers. Other customers and the pub landlord now fixed him with disapproving looks. Some jeered and others laughed. The man rushed across the bar floor and into the street, the door slamming behind him.

Felicity gave me one of her disapproving looks. 'Archie, I know you were trying to act in a most gallant way in defending my honour, but did you have to use such dreadful language?'

I moved closer to her and quickly kissed her on the forehead. 'Sorry, darling, please forgive me. Sometimes one has to fight fire with fire,' I said softly, with passion in my voice.

The other customers soon forgot the incident and somebody fed more money into the jukebox, resulting in the sound of Harry James trumpeting and Dick Haymes singing, 'Here Comes the Night'. Time for us to be pushing off soon, I thought, with other things on my mind.

The landlord moved across to the bar in front of us.

'Did I hear you mention that it was your wedding anniversary today?' he asked, treating us to a friendly smile.

Felicity gave the landlord one of her delicious smiles. 'Yes, it is, our first, and we were enjoying our little celebration until that dreadful, boorish lout started annoying us.'

The landlord gave a sympathetic nod. 'Yes, I'm sorry about that. I'm afraid he's a bad lot. I've warned him several times about his insulting behaviour and, after his appalling conduct tonight—peeing all over the floor—while I'm the landlord he'll not be drinking in The Pig and Whistle again. Now, what can I get for you two lovebirds? It's on the house.'

'My wife would like a double gin and lime and I was just about to order a double whisky when you came over to us,' I answered for us both.

The landlord grinned, knowingly. 'Then that's what it'll be,' he said, as he pushed Felicity's glass up against the gin bottle's optic.

We stayed for about another hour, or it might have been two, when we finally lurched out of the pub and headed up the street, me leading the way to the nearest fish and chip shop.

'This is hardly what I expected when you said you would take me for a meal after we had drinks in the pub,' said Felicity, standing back from the door of the fish and chip shop.

'Oh, come on, don't be so stuffy. It'll be a new experience for you. You stay here if you don't want to come in while I order our supper.'

'Do you mean we have to eat it out on the street, without proper plates and cutlery?'

'Of course, it's the only way to eat fish and chips, in newspaper, with loads of salt and vinegar—and fingers were made before forks.'

Felicity shrugged her shoulders and her hunger won. 'Oh, very well, I'll try anything once,' she said resignedly as she joined me in the warmth of the shop.

We ate our fish and chip supper sitting on the deck of the ferry crossing back to South Woolwich.

'Well, I have to admit, although it might have been because I hadn't eaten since lunchtime, I really enjoyed those fish and chips,' Felicity said as she wiped her hands on my handkerchief.

'Good, I knew you would. Now then, what's next? How late can you stop out without causing a ruckus at home?'

'Actually I told my parents that I was visiting my friend Peggy and would be staying overnight at her home tonight.'

'That's good. If we have a slow walk back to my house, my mother and stepfather will be fast asleep by the time we get there; we can spend the night together in my room.' I tried to sound as though I was inviting someone to my home for afternoon tea and biscuits.

Felicity looked doubtful. 'Won't your parents hear us when we climb up the stairs and pass their bedroom?'

'No, not if we take our shoes off and creep up quietly,' I said, with the confidence of someone who was practised in moving up stairs without disturbing the other occupants of the house.

It was a little after eleven o'clock when we arrived at my house, which was in darkness. I quietly eased my key into the lock and turned it without a sound. I opened the door and we entered and took our shoes off in the hall. Carrying our shoes, I led the way soundlessly. We reached the first floor landing and Felicity stood still outside the lavatory. 'I need to go to the loo,' she whispered, as she opened the lavatory door and disappeared into the room.

'Don't pull the chain,' I whispered back with a trace of panic in my voice.

Felicity did what she had to do in silence. 'You see, I can be as quiet as you when it comes to sneaking in and out of houses,' she said as she emerged from the lavatory. 'But the men in your house should be reminded to put the seat down after they've used the loo.'

'Yes, my mother's always reminding our lodger about that. That's his room,' I whispered, as we passed a door on the second landing. 'He fought against the Japanese in Burma and is always having nightmares. He shouts out in the middle of the night, things like, "Fetch some more grenades, the little yellow bastards are swarming all over our positions".'

'How awful for the poor man,' Felicity whispered.

We reached the top landing and were about to enter my attic bedroom when Felicity somehow caught her high-heeled shoes in the banisters. She let go of the shoes and they fell clattering down the stairs and hit my mother's bedroom door before they came to rest.

'Stay quiet, I'll go down and get them,' I whispered, and started creeping back down the stairs.

I was just about to pick them up from the floor when my stepfather, Eddie, called out from the bedroom. 'Is that you, Archie? What time do you call this to come home?'

'Sorry Eddie, I missed the last bus and had to walk from Eltham. Goodnight.'

I rejoined Felicity on the landing and we entered my attic bedroom. I didn't put on the light. The moonlight afforded enough light for us to get undressed and slip between the ice-cold sheets of my bed. Felicity, who always felt the cold, clung to me for warmth.

'Crikey, you feel like a block of ice,' I said, as I started to rub Felicity's arms and legs.

Felicity shivered. 'Please rub my back now, I feel frozen. However do you sleep in this cold room without any heating, or even a hot water bottle?'

'I've got used to it. Anyway I'm hot-blooded,' I said, as my hands continued to gently rub Felicity's back and thighs, and lewd thoughts were entering my mind.

'What happens in the morning?' asked Felicity in a sleepy voice.

'We'll creep back down the stairs about six o'clock. Nobody is working tomorrow so they'll have a lie in. We can then go into Woolwich to get some breakfast before we catch a bus to take you back home. Your mum and dad won't be up and it doesn't matter if they are. They'll think you've just caught a bus back from Peggy's place and...'

It was then that Felicity started snoring and I realised I was talking to myself.

$$* \quad * \quad * \quad *$$

'I suppose this is another of your fine dining restaurants,' complained Felicity, as we entered what was known locally as The Riverside Greasy Spoon Café.

'Oh, it's not that bad. I picked it because it's not far from your bus stop. We haven't got too much time to look around for somewhere else that suits your ladyship. Anyway, they do a smashing whale meat stew and the tea is always hot, strong and sweet, just like me,' I enthused.

Felicity settled for a dried egg omelette and toast. I favoured a bacon sandwich, which proved to be more sandwich than bacon. The food and a strong cup of tea helped us feel more awake after our short night's sleep, and the hasty, but silent, retreat from my house, unwashed and dishevelled, for the 20-minute walk into town. I accompanied Felicity on her bus home and watched her as she let herself into the house before I left to walk back home.

Ambling across the common it occurred to me that I had spent more than I had intended or could afford. I took out my wallet—no folding money in that. I checked the loose change in my pocket and found about two shillings and fourpence—enough for a packet of fags and my train fare on Monday. I was in deep trouble as I had spent nearly all my wages. I had nothing to give my mother for housekeeping or to pay my fares the following week. No doubt about it, I'd be up the creek without a paddle unless I could get my hands on a couple of quid that weekend. It suddenly came to me that I could say I had lost my pay packet somewhere on my way home. Now who would believe that story and give, or lend, me enough to cover my loss?

The only person I knew who had any real money was my grandmother. She was a shrewd old bird, the sort who'd smell a con a mile off, but she did have lots of money. She'd won about 10,000 pounds on Littlewoods Football Pools two or three years ago, and had spent little of it on any of her children, let alone her grandchildren, but in my circumstances, surely she'd come across with a couple of quid. It was worth a try.

'Hello, Archie, what on earth are you doing out at this time on a Saturday morning?' asked my grandmother as she opened the front door to me. 'Come in, but make sure you wipe your feet.'

'Hello, Gran,' I said, as I made a great play of wiping my feet on the doormat. 'How are your legs? Not playing up again, are they?'

'They're no better for you asking, but since you're here, you could run a few errands for me. I want seven pounds of King Edwards, don't pay more than sixpence for them; a large cabbage, make sure it's fresh and hearty, and a pound of carrots. I'm not paying for dirt so scrape the mud off them before they are weighed. Oh yes, and two cottage loaves—make sure they are fresh. You'll need to take some bread units with you and—'

'Gran,' I interrupted, 'I've been up all night looking for my wallet, the one that Uncle Bernard brought back from Egypt for me. I lost it somewhere on the way home from work last evening. It had all my wages in it. I've got no money to give my mother,' I said, in an exaggerated plaintive voice.

'My word, Archie, you are in a state. I can see by your eyes that you've had little sleep last night and you do look as though you need a wash and shave, but why are you telling me all this? Shouldn't you be telling your mother?'

'To be honest, Gran, I was hoping that *you* might let me have some money to cover my loss. I *must* pay my mother. You know how much she relies on my weekly contribution to the housekeeping, and then there are my train fares for next week. If you can help me I'll do that painting you want done in your back bedroom.'

My grandmother looked at me like a detective about to start questioning a criminal suspect.

'Have you reported the loss to the railway police? It might have been found and handed in to them.'

'No, but I'm sure I had the wallet with me when I got off the train because I remember putting my season ticket back in it when I passed the barrier.'

'But I thought you said that you had no money for fares next week. If you've got a season ticket you'll not need money for them, will you?'

This wasn't going to be easy. 'It was a weekly ticket, which expired yesterday. I'll need to get another one on Monday morning.' A neat parry, I thought.

'Well, how much did you lose, in total?'

'My two pounds wages,' why not make it worthwhile, I thought, 'and my annual bonus—30 shillings. Major Carlton-Smythe pays it in November so that we can use it for buying Christmas presents.' I was beginning to think that lying was becoming too easy.

Gran gave me her interrogative look again.

'So what you're saying is that you lost three pounds ten shillings in all.'

'Yes, that's right, Gran.'

'Hmm…that's certainly a serious loss, one you can ill afford, but there is always the chance that your wallet has been found by an honest person who has handed it in at the police station. You must report the matter to the police.'

'Yes Gran, I will, but I need the money to pay my mother today. I usually give it to her on Friday evening, but I haven't seen her since yesterday morning, so she'll be wondering what has happened to me, and her money.'

My grandmother didn't respond, but just sat looking at me with her disquieting fixed stare, as if reading my innermost thoughts. That was worrying for me and I found it hard not to betray my guilty feelings by fidgeting in my chair or averting my gaze. Suddenly she got up from her chair and, to my relief, picked up her large leather handbag from the sideboard. She opened the handbag and withdrew a worn leather purse, opened it and peered at its contents.

'I only have three pounds to spare at the moment. I shall need some money for you to do those errands I mentioned when you arrived.'

Cunning old bird, I thought, but said: 'Three pounds would be a great help, Gran. I can pay my mother and have enough for my fares, and have a little left over to save up for Christmas presents.'

My grandmother handed me the three pound notes and a half a crown coin.

'The half-crown is for the shopping. I'll write you a note of what I want.'

'That won't be necessary, Gran, I can remember what you want: seven pounds of King Edward's potatoes, at no more than sixpence; a fresh and hearty cabbage; dirt-free carrots and fresh baked bread,' I unhesitatingly reeled off. 'Oh yes, and I'll need some bread units.'

'Good boy, you remembered. Here are the bread units. Off you go and make sure you get the right change. That greengrocer is always trying to get away with fiddling with dodgy scales and short-changing his customers. I wouldn't shop there, but it's as far as I can walk with my bad legs.'

'Don't worry, Gran, he'll not cheat me. I'll be back in a flash with exactly what you want and the correct change. Trust me.'

My grandmother let me out of the front door and as I walked down the steps to the pavement, called out: 'Archie, you'll not forget you promised to paint my back bedroom. While you're at it, you might as well paint the hall, stairs and landing.'

Bloody hell, she certainly wants her pound of flesh, I thought, but turned and smiled. 'It'll be done, Gran, as soon as I can get around to it,' I said, and gave her what was intended to be a reassuring wave as I hurried off to do her shopping.

CHAPTER 18

▼

It was the second week in December and my thoughts were turning to what Christmas presents I could afford to buy. Felicity's gift was my top priority; then there was my mother's and Eddie's presents to consider. Cigarettes would probably be OK for them. Dennis, the lodger, and my best friend Cyril, would probably appreciate the same. Presents for my maternal grandparents were no problem; I'd finish off painting their bedroom and stairs and landing, and dig over the back garden. The rest of the family would have to be satisfied with Christmas cards. I still had a box of Christmas cards I had brought away with me when I left the print shop two years earlier. The cards had been incorrectly folded and were unacceptable for sale. I was told to put them all in the paper salvage bins, but salvaged a couple of boxes for my own use.

'Have you finished all today's amendments?' Humbledick asked, awaking me from my daydreaming about Christmas.

'Oh yes, nearly all finished,' I said, pulling a file of cablegrams from my in tray. 'I was just wondering what days we would be getting off for the Christmas holiday this year.'

'Don't talk to me about Christmas. That's all my wife's been on about for weeks. She thinks that because the war has been over for more than two years the shops should now be full of goods. I've tried to explain to her that we are in for a few more years of rationing, tightening our belts and putting up with austerity measures before the country is fully back on its feet.'

I stifled a yawn with my hand and reached for my packet of Player's Weights. Humbledick took the hint and paused, pushed his accounts books to one side and filled his pipe. I guessed he was in the mood for talking.

'Another thing that is making her life miserable, is that there is a baby boom going on all over the country at the moment. More kids than ever are being born, but she still can't get pregnant. Of course, like a woman would, she blames me. Says I'm "not doing it right". I just don't know what I'm doing wrong. I've tried every position in the book, and nothing works.'

'What book is that? I didn't know they published books that told you how to perform the sex act. Where do you get them?'

Humbledick laughed. 'I was speaking figuratively; I've never seen such books on sale. I only wish there were.'

Time, I thought, to get Humbledick off his favourite topic. 'About those Christmas holidays…'

'Sorry, I digressed,' said Humbledick, looking up at the calendar on the wall next to his desk. 'As Christmas Day falls on a Thursday, we'll be off that day and on Friday, which is Boxing Day. That'll make a rather nice break from work.'

'Do you think the major will let us pack up at lunchtime on Christmas Eve? That'll be the last chance we'll get to do any Christmas shopping,' I said.

Humbledick frowned. 'I shouldn't think so and if he does it will be the first time he has. Anyway, Christmas is always a busy time in the office. Not so much during the war years, but before the war the major would go out buying scores of Christmas presents for all the shipowners who held contracts with our principals. I know he intends to do the same thing this year. It'll mean a lot of parcel wrapping. Just the job for you, since you say you are so good at wrapping parcels.'

'Do you mean that he buys presents for all the shipowners? They're all rich! Some are millionaires and he buys presents for them? It's unbelievable!'

'I don't agree with it myself; to me it smacks of bribery, but it is the done thing in the business world. The major uses it as a sort of "sweetener" before he goes around to the shipowners in the New Year to get them to renew their annual contracts with our principals.'

'How much does he spend on each present?' I ventured.

'It can vary, but he usually spends about five shillings on each,' replied Humbledick.

'That's not much to spend on a present for a millionaire. Surely a five shilling present isn't enough to influence them into signing a contract,' I said.

'I must say you do seem very interested in the major's Christmas shopping habits. What you have to understand is that he is only sending token presents to the shipowners, but it does seem to work and the greater majority of them renew their contracts every year. Now, I think we've talked enough about the major's Christmas presents and it's time to get back to work,' said Humbledick, reaching for his cash books.

'Just one more question; does the major ever buy his staff Christmas presents?'

'No, certainly not in all the time I've worked for him. Now drop the subject and get on with some work. If he were to walk in and see us slacking, we'd probably get the sack for Christmas, and it wouldn't be Santa's sack,' said Humbledick, with a forced laugh.

I resumed my work, but my mind was concentrating on the possibility that there might be an opportunity for me to benefit from the information I had gleaned from Humbledick about the major's purchase of Christmas presents.

*   *   *   *

'Ho, ho, ho and good morning!' bellowed the major as he burst into the office carrying a large suitcase.

Mrs Carlton-Smythe, with a pained expression on her face, followed him into the office. Humbledick and I both jumped to attention and shouted back:

'Good morning, sir, good morning, Mrs Carlton-Smythe.'

Mrs Carlton-Smythe looked more embarrassed than usual by our parade-ground performance. She, like us, probably thought the major a most unlikely Father Christmas, but it would be better to humour the silly old goat. He might have something in that case for his loyal, hard-working staff, but my guess was that he didn't. The major placed the case on the floor in the corner of the office. 'Humbledick, I want the boxes of cigarettes and books in that case wrapped up and dispatched as soon as possible, or sooner. Mrs Carlton-Smythe has put some special greetings cards, Christmas paper, brown paper and a roll of gummed brown paper in the case. All you've got to do is get them wrapped up and posted tonight. There's a list of all the people and their addresses, and against each name is the brand of cigarette or the title of the book they are to receive. Make sure the address labels are neatly typed and that the greetings cards are placed in the parcels.'

I pricked up my ears—this sounded promising.

'Yes, sir, you can leave it to me to see that they are all neatly wrapped and dispatched with the evening's post,' said Humbledick, giving me a look that could only mean that I would be getting the job.

'Fine, that's fine,' said the major, looking at his watch. 'I'm not going to be doing anything in the office today, so if you have anything that requires my signature, or urgent attention, let me see it now. My wife and I will be staying in town tonight, probably at the Dorchester. We've been invited to a special dinner party organised by the London-based ship-owners. It's something I must attend. There could be an opportunity to secure some new contracts for next year.'

'Yes, sir, you're probably right. It's surprising what a good meal and a few drinks can do to make businessmen more susceptible to gentle persuasion. I do hope you both have a very enjoyable evening and that you are successful in obtaining some new contracts.'

Cripes! Humbledick is certainly in his best crawling form today, I thought. Mrs Carlton-Smythe smiled at me and gave me a questioning look, which I guessed meant: 'Have you any clothing coupons for me, Archie?' I answered her with a smile and a gentle shake of my head.

The major and Mrs Carlton-Smythe moved towards the door. 'Well, if you've nothing of consequence to report and nothing for my attention, we'll be off to lunch. Remember, I shan't be in the office until the New Year, when I shall need all the contracts ready to take out for renewal. See that they are ready, Humbledick,' added the major, as he closed the office door.

Five seconds later the office door opened and the major, his face redder than usual, popped his head around the door. 'Oh, just one thing more, a merry Christmas and a happy New Year to you both.'

I bet Mrs Carlton-Smythe reminded him, I thought.

'Thank you very much, sir, and a merry Christmas to you and Mrs Carlton-Smythe, and I sincerely hope that you both enjoy good health, happiness and prosperity in the coming year.'

'Creep,' I muttered inaudibly.

The Carlton-Smythes gone, Humbledick gave a deep sigh, sat at his desk and stuffed tobacco into his pipe. I took advantage of the lull in activity and lit a cigarette.

'Don't get too comfortable, Archie,' admonished Humbledick through a cloud of pipe smoke. 'You've got a lot of parcels to wrap up, but then you're good at that aren't you, or so you keep telling me.'

'That's one thing I can do well—wrap up parcels. Wrapping up boxes of cigarettes and books is a doddle for someone like me who has made a tidy parcel of everything from a stuffed owl to a crystal chandelier when I worked at the pawnbrokers.'

'Good, then you'd better get cracking now. There's a lot to be done in a short time if we are to catch the evening post,' said Humbledick, as he handed me the list of addressees. 'I should type the address labels first, then sort out what is to go to whom, and pencil on each wrapped parcel the name of the intended recipient then, finally, stick on the labels. Of course, you'll need to weigh the parcels. You'll only need to weigh one box of cigarettes because they will all weigh the same, but the books are of different sizes, so you'll need to weigh them all. When you've done that, work out the postage and I'll let you have the exact money from the petty cash.'

'Yes, Mr Humbledick, you've nothing to worry about, I'll have them ready for the evening post, trust me,' I said, beginning to realise that I was about to carry out one of my most rewarding coups. It was lucky I had two full packets of chewing gum in my desk drawer.

Humbledick went out to lunch, which gave me plenty of time to type out the labels I needed for my own use. These labels would be stuck over the other labels on the selected parcels of cigarettes and books when I took them to the post office.

I examined all the cigarettes; they were all the more expensive brands. I earmarked Players Navy Cut and Senior Service for my mother, Eddie,

Dennis, the lodger, and Cyril, and selected a box of Balkan Sobranie for myself. Next the books, which included *The Iceman Cometh, All the King's Men, The White Goddess, The Winslow Boy,* and *An Inspector Calls,* none of which, at first sight, appealed to me. The one that caught my attention was a Saint book, Leslie Charteris's latest, which I hadn't read, *The Saint Sees it Through.* I could read it before Christmas and pass it on to Cyril for his birthday, which was three days after Christmas—on Innocents' Day. Cyril, an innocent? What a joke!

By the time Humbledick came back from lunch I had typed all the address labels and packed nearly half the parcels.

'My, my, you *have* been busy. You'd better slip off now for a quick lunch,' said Humbledick.

'No, I'm OK, I'll get these finished and leave a bit earlier, if that's all right with you. I could go on home after I've dropped them off at the post office.'

'Yes, by all means, do that, but what about the suitcase? You won't want to take that home, will you?'

'No, I'll nip back with it before I go home.'

By about three thirty I had wrapped and weighed the parcels, stuck on the labels and presented Humbledick with a note of the postage required. Humbledick looked at my note, picked out a parcel from the suitcase and placed it on the scales. 'Just checking as it's very easy to make a mistake when weighing items for postage, but I see you've got the price bang on.'

'Do you want to weigh any more?' I asked, trying not to sound sarcastic.

'No, that's all right, here's the money,' Humbledick replied as he handed me a sheaf of pound notes.

I pocketed the money and closed the suitcase. There was just one more thing to do before I left the office; remove the chewing gum from underneath the weighing platform of the scales.

'I do believe that Daphne Weldunn is looking down into the office again,' I said, looking up at the third floor window.

As Humbledick turned to look up at the window, I deftly plucked the much larger than usual piece of chewing gum from the scales and stuck it under my desk.

'I didn't see her,' said Humbledick in a disappointed voice.

'Oh, I must have been mistaken. It was probably some other girl who looks a bit like Daphne having a crafty dekko down here. I'm off then,' I said, grabbing the case and walking out of the door.

The post office was crowded, so I took the suitcase around to the near empty ABC restaurant, ordered a cup of tea and sat at a corner table away from the few other customers. I opened the suitcase under the table and removed the parcels I had marked with a pencilled cross and stuck my Christmas present labels over the original labels that had been stuck on in the office. I then made a list of the number and value of stamps I would require to buy at the post office. I tore up the list I had made up in the office and deposited the pieces in a waste bin.

When I had finished my tea and smoked a cigarette, I went back to the post office, which was still crowded. When it came to my turn I handed the counter clerk my list of required stamps and enough of the cash Humbledick had given me, to pay for the stamps.

'Now that's what I like to see—someone with a bit of gumption to weigh the parcels and work out their postage before he brings them to the post office; but I'll have to weigh some of the variously sized parcels. You wouldn't want your addressees to have to pay surcharges on their parcels because of there being insufficient postage on them, would you?'

'No, I certainly wouldn't,' I said, and meant it.

The clerk passed the stamps and change over the counter to me and I spent several minutes sticking stamps on the parcels. Thirsty work, but I was comforted by the thought that my little postage fiddle had netted me a nice profit and I could call into the station buffet for a pint of shandy before I caught my train home.

I returned to the office with the empty suitcase. Humbledick was sitting at his desk reading the *Daily Chronicle* and smoking his pipe. 'Get them all away OK?'

'Yes, there'll be a few happy people when they receive their parcels in a couple of days' time. I suppose even millionaires get excited when they receive a surprise parcel at Christmas time,' I said, knowing of at least one person who would be more than happy to receive his.

'Yes, I'm sure you're right,' said Humbledick, as he started to clear his desk to go home.

*   *   *   *

'You'll never guess what came in the post this morning, Archie,' said my mother, as she placed a larger than usual portion of her meat and vegetable pie on my plate. 'Five parcels, one each for Eddie, Dennis and me, and two for you. I've opened mine; it had a box of 50 Players cigarettes in it. The others all look like they've got boxes of cigarettes in them as well. One of yours is heavier, feels like a book. I've left them on the occasional table in the sitting room.'

'Who sent them, Santa Claus?' I said, with a laugh.

'I bet it was you, Archie; it's the sort of thing you'd do, send surprise parcels to people at Christmas. If it was you, why did you buy expensive cigarettes? Player's Weights would have been just as appreciated.'

'No, it wasn't me and I'd hardly be likely to send parcels to myself, would I? Didn't the parcel have a card in it?'

'No, there was nothing to indicate who'd sent it, but the parcels were all franked at Fenchurch Street Post Office, which is near where you work, isn't it?'

'Yes, but I don't know anything about them. Can't you just accept that Father Christmas had your names on his list this year?'

'Yes, that's what I'll do, Archie, but thanks anyway, you're a son in a million,' she said, as she kissed my forehead.

I smiled and responded in the best way I could. 'This pie is just great, but it's a pity there's so little meat in it.' Never mind, I thought, I have plenty of cash for the weekend. On Saturday morning I'll take Cyril out to Manzies for a slap-up meal of pie and mash. I'm looking forward to giving the blonde counter assistant my over-used and facetious order, 'Double pie and mash four times twice please and put plenty of gravy on it.' She would just laugh and say, 'It's you two silly bleeders, again, trying to get me all confused.'

On Saturday afternoon I'll take Felicity out for a stroll in the woods and once again try to get her to abandon her chastity. Some hope, I know, but she is well worth trying it on. On Sunday afternoon I'll buy her the biggest box of chocolates my saved up sweet coupons will allow and help her eat them while we watch Humphrey Bogart and Ida Lupino in a rerun of *High Sierra*.

Life sometimes had its better moments.

CHAPTER 19

▼

The brown envelope, marked 'OHMS', came a few days before my eighteenth birthday. I was expecting it since I received a previous letter, which gave me the opportunity to choose the service in which I would like to do my national service.

The Royal Navy was doing well for regular recruits, so there were few openings for national servicemen. Anyway, if there had been, I wouldn't have wanted to spend my time in such cramped conditions aboard a naval ship and sleep in one of those ridiculous hammocks. I'd tried one out in an uncle's garden and fallen out of it too many times to have enjoyed the experience. So, the choice was either the army or the RAF. I chose the RAF as it seemed the more glamorous of the two services, and I had heard from several people who had served in the army that there was a lot more 'bull' to put up with there than in the RAF.

The letter instructed me to report to RAF Padgate before 1200 hours, on Wednesday, 21st April 1948. This meant that I had about two or three more months of freedom. To make the most of this time I needed money and, although I had received another five shillings a week pay rise from Major Carlton-Smythe, I was still finding it diffi-

cult to manage without my little moneymaking fiddles. Since my coup
at Christmas, times had been lean and there had been little opportunity to raise any cash by my usual means.

Perhaps it was time to leave Carlton-Smythe's and look for a temporary local job that might be nearer home and pay more. An answer to
my problem came unexpectedly a few days later when I shared the dining table with Eddie—he got home earlier than me in the winter—
when he mentioned that he had started with a new firm. They were
engaged in repairing the bomb damaged London docks. The work he
was doing was constructing wooden shuttering; into which was poured
concrete to set before shuttering was removed.

'Is your firm taking on any more workers, Eddie?' I enquired.

'Yes, they are. They can't get enough men to do the job. I'm supposed to have a full-time mate, but usually I have to work without one.
It's bloody hard work, but they do pay a couple of coppers above the
normal rates and there's plenty of overtime if you want. Of course, at
this time of the year, the overtime has to be worked at weekends.'

'What is the hourly rate for labourers?'

'That would be one shilling and eight pence.'

I quickly calculated 44 hours—my weekends were too precious to
be spent at work—at one and eight an hour, which amounted to about
£3.13.4d. Not bad, not bad at all, and only a few coppers bus or tram
fares to get to work.

'Are there any fiddles to make extra money, Eddie?' I asked, fast
coming to the decision that I would apply for a job with Eddie's firm
for the weeks I had left in Civvy Street.

'No, I'm not aware of any moneymaking fiddles. The bloke who
runs the tea swindle probably makes a few coppers a week out of it. He
charges everyone a shilling a week. For that they get two cups of tea on
Monday to Friday and one cup on Saturday morning. He never works

overtime, so perhaps he does make quite a bit from the tea-making job.'

'That's it then, is it?'

'Yes, I guess so, but I think the concreting ganger is a runner for a bookmaker because he's always taking bets from the blokes.'

'So the blokes like to gamble, do they?' I said, an idea beginning to form in my mind.

'They certainly do. Some of the men gamble every day on horses, dogs and anything else that's going on at the time.'

'Do you reckon your boss would take me on as a labourer with your gang?'

'I'm sure he would, and if he did you could work as my mate. I know you can use a hammer and saw, and can measure lengths of wood, so you'd do fine. When you're ready to start, come in with me and I'll take you to the site foreman's office. He takes on all the new workers.'

'Thanks, Eddie, I'll let you know as soon as I've given my notice with Keith Carlton-Smythe's.'

Now where did I put that Crown and Anchor board and dice when the Dark Town Gambling Club closed down?

*   *   *   *

'I thought you ought to know straight away, Mr Humbledick, I've received my calling up papers and I am shortly going into the RAF for a couple of years. I expect you'll need me to give you plenty of notice, to give you time to recruit another lad to take over as your assistant.'

'When do you have to leave?'

'In a few weeks' time.'

I thought it better not to tell him the exact date, as he'd probably expect me to stay on until then.

'You can stay on as long as you like, Archie. You're weekly paid so you only need to give a week's notice, but I would like you to stay on for a week to train the new lad we recruit. I'm sure the major would be grateful if you did and probably give you a small bonus for doing it.'

'Well, let's say I'm leaving a week after you take on a new lad, then.'

The thought of the bonus decided me to be as helpful as I could. After all, Humbledick had gone to bat for me when I had been caught fiddling.

'Yes, that'll be fine. I'll let the major know you are leaving and get on to the local labour exchanges to see if they've got any suitable people on their books. In the meantime, I would much appreciate it if you would ensure that all the contracts for the New Year are kept fully amended until you leave. Major Carlton-Smythe will be taking them out to the shipowners at the end of this month and he'd not be very happy if the prices weren't up to date.'

'No problem at all, I'm bang up to date at the moment and will see to it that I stay that way until I leave. You can depend on me, Mr Humbledick,' I said.

'Thanks, Archie; I thought you'd take that line. I know you've been pinching the major's cigarettes, and you've worked on more fiddles than Antonio Stradivarius since you've been here, but you've always done a good job for us and you'll be missed. I hope you enjoy your national service and come to see us when you're demobbed. I can't promise to hold your job open for you, but we'd always be glad to see you.'

I looked at the sad-faced Humbledick and realised he had been sincere in what he had said. 'Thanks, Charles,' I said, daring to use his first name, something I had never done in the two years I had known him. 'I shall certainly remember you and the major, and will pop in to see you when I've finished my national service.'

*   *   *   *

I called on Felicity that evening to give her the news about my call up and plans for changing my job. She wasn't pleased to hear what I had to say. 'So, you're going into the RAF then. Some might call that the 'soft option' when our army is currently serving in trouble spots all around the world.'

'Hold on, you're quite wrong about the RAF being a soft option. The RAF is deployed in most of the places where the army is serving. In wartime, RAF personnel can be exposed to danger just as much as soldiers. Even those airmen who do not serve as aircrew can be involved in a combat role, and all airmen, apart from the medical personnel, whatever their primary ground duties, are trained for combat and may be called upon to defend their airfields against enemy attack from both ground and air forces. The RAF even has its own regiment of infantry and light anti-aircraft trained men to take the offensive against enemy regular troops and guerrilla forces threatening RAF airfields.'

Felicity looked at me with awe. 'Oh, I'm sorry, Archie, I didn't realise that airmen sometimes have to fight like soldiers. I suppose my uncles, who were always telling me that the RAF had an easy time during the war, influenced me.'

My study of RAF recruiting literature was certainly paying off.

'Oh well, whatever you end up in, navy, army or air force, national service could be the best thing that could happen to you. I know that I shall miss you when you are away, but a temporary separation might be the best thing for us. I'm sure you'll disagree with what I have to say, but I honestly consider that you are fast becoming a rather self-centred spiv, with little else on your mind, but how to make a quick quid and having your evil way with any girl weak enough to let you get the better of them.'

I felt hurt by Felicity's criticism, but laughed, took her into my arms and kissed her.

'See what I mean?' Felicity said, as she pulled away from me.

'I'm sorry, darling, but it is for you that I try to make money, so that I might be able to treat you to the things you deserve,' I said, as I pulled her back and gave her a passionate kiss.

She responded and I took advantage of the moment to attempt a more daring approach to our canoodling.

'You sexy beast!' she cried, as she tried to pull away from me again. 'You're just after my body!'

I released my hold on her and we sat down on a nearby park bench.

'I haven't finished with you yet, Archie. What on earth were you thinking about, leaving Keith Carlton-Smythe's agency for a job as a labourer?'

I had anticipated that she would ask this question and knew that my excuse for taking on the new job simply because the pay was better, would only confirm what she had been saying.

'It was to help Eddie. His firm couldn't get enough men to finish an important repair job on the docks and he needed a mate to work with him. I'll only be with them for two or three months and there's less travelling involved in getting to work, which will mean a saving in train fares.'

Felicity wasn't impressed by my excuse and shrugged her shoulders.

'Well, I still think it is a backwards move, but I'll say no more about it, although I do hope it won't mean you turning up at my house wearing a workman's cap, overalls and muddy clodhoppers.'

I laughed and squeezed her hand. 'Of course not, darling, I wouldn't dare show myself on the street dressed like that.'

We both laughed out loud and I knew that things were right with us again.

CHAPTER 20

▼

'This is Archie, Archie Cholmondeley; the lad I was telling you about, Mr Fothersgill,' said Eddie, introducing me to the site foreman.

I had asked Eddie not to describe me as his stepson, thinking the site foreman might suspect him of being a bit nepotistic (a word I had gleaned from my nightly read of the *Oxford Dictionary*) on my behalf.

Fothersgill, a big, balding, bluff looking man in his fifties, leaned over his desk and looked me over. I pulled myself up to my full height and smiled.

'Sit yourselves down,' he said with a wave of his arm at two chairs in the corner of the office. 'Well, you've recommended him, Eddie, so give me good reason to take him on.'

Eddie, unaccustomed to making off-the-cuff statements, paused, looking appealingly at me. I didn't say anything, but gave him an encouraging look. We'd agreed beforehand that he should do all the talking about my experience because he knew the site foreman and what he would want to hear about me.

'Well, Eddie, what sort of experience has he had in the building industry?' asked Fothersgill, impatiently.

Eddie suddenly became alert and leaned forwards in his chair. 'He's laboured for brickies, chippies, slaters and tilers, painters, plasterers and plumbers. He can knock up a good mix of compo, bang a nail in straight, saw a straight line, put up a plasterboard ceiling, tile a kitchen, glaze a window, hang a door, slate a roof, mend a burst pipe and whatever else he's asked to do. He's bright, polite, strong as an ox, not afraid of hard work and can make a good cup of tea.'

'Gorblimey, Eddie, you make him sound like bloody Superman in dungarees. Is there anything he *can't* do?'

'I suppose there's lots he can't do, but if he can't do something he'll always give it a damned good try before he gives up on it,' replied Eddie, with feeling.

Fothersgill turned to me and grinned. 'Eddie has certainly given you high praise. Let's hope you can live up to it. By the way, how old are you?'

'As a matter of fact, I'm 18 today.'

'Well, if you get nothing else for your birthday, you've got yourself a job,' said Fothersgill, with a broad grin. 'Have you got your insurance cards with you?'

'Yes, and my income tax form P45,' I replied confidently.

'Good, then you can start here on Monday, eight o'clock sharp, as Eddie's mate. Just one thing though: for Pete's sake don't come to work dressed as you are. You look more like a bloody stockbroker than a chippie's mate.'

'Thank you, Mr Fothersgill, please be assured I shall be here promptly at eight o'clock on Monday, and will be appropriately attired,' I retorted, with deliberate pomposity.

'Where did you find him, Eddie? He even *talks* like a bloody stockbroker.'

'Well, he did work for a couple of years in a shipping office and mixed with a lot of shipping *magnates,* so perhaps he was *attracted* to their posh way of speaking,' said Eddie, with an out-of-character attempt at humour.

'OK, that's enough, Eddie; time to get back to work. We're a couple of weeks behind schedule and can't afford to waste any more time chatting. Perhaps with this young man of many talents to help you, you'll have the north end ramp shuttered and ready for concreting by the end of next week.'

Eddie took the hint and quickly ushered me out of the site foreman's office, for him to get back to his shuttering and me to search for the nearest Army and Navy store to buy some appropriate clothing for Monday.

*   *   *   *

Eddie gave me an early call on Monday and we set off together by tram for the docks. I didn't wear my overalls, but carried them in an old canvass bag, mainly because I didn't want the neighbours, or anyone I knew, especially Ramsbottom, seeing me on my way to work wearing overalls.

Eddie took me to the site workers' hut, where the workmen gathered at break times for their tea, and to eat their sandwiches at lunchtime.

'You can leave your jacket and bag in here; it'll be quite safe, but don't leave any money in the pockets. We've had the odd case of pilfering in the past,' advised Eddie.

'Thanks for the tip, Eddie, I'll bear it mind when I've got some cash to safeguard.

Having become unaccustomed to heavy physical work during my two-year employment at Keith Carlton-Smythe's, I was glad when break time came and we left our workplace for the ten-minute tea break in the site hut. The tea was made, and the old boy who made it collected my shilling for the week. Eddie introduced me to most of the workmen who came to the hut and the ten-minute break soon stretched to 20 minutes, before a chargehand came into the hut and called us all out and back to work.

At lunchtime Eddie and I sat together eating our sandwiches and listening to the banter of the assembled workers. Eddie rarely joined in their conversation, which was mainly about horse racing, or the problems they were experiencing with their wives or children.

'That bleedin' "Blue Peter" let me down for a six-race accumulator. If he'd 'ave come in I wouldn't 'ave been here now. I'd 'ave won enuff to 'ave stayed at 'ome for a year,' moaned one.

'I know, it's a sod when that 'appens,' said another. 'I've had a bloody awful week. I 'aven't picked a winner for days. I suppose Jack Mallick will be in 'ere in a minute asking for our bets. What do you fancy at Cheltenham this afternoon?'

'Dunno, with my effing luck, I wouldn't try to guess.'

'I've got my money on "Sydney's Pride", in the four fifteen at Cheltenham,' called out an unmistakable Australian voice from across the room.

'You must be bloody crazy, Ozzie, that bloody nag's worse than a three-legged donkey. It ain't got a cat in 'ell's chance of getting around the course, never mind winning the race,' shouted back the loser on "Blue Peter".

'Don't you be so sure, Cobber. Anyway, I like backing rank outsiders. When they *do* come in the winnings are worth picking up,' Ozzie retorted with a laugh.

The restroom door opened with a bang and in strode Jack Mallick, the chargehand concreter, and part-time bookie's runner.

'Any bets today, lads? If you haven't, it's time you lot were back on the job.'

'Yes, Jacko, stick me ten bob on "Sydney's Pride" to win in the four fifteen at Cheltenham today,' said Ozzie, handing Mallick a ten-shilling note and a slip of scribbled on paper, torn from the edge of the *Sporting Life*.

'So, you're still backing outsiders, Ozzie? Won't you ever learn? That's what keeps bookies in business, sucker punters like you backing outsiders,' said Mallick, with a sneer, which made his face look uglier than it was.

'You should worry about what I bet on. You get your commission from the bookie you're running for, so what's it to you what I bet on?' Ozzie replied sharply.

Mallick snatched the ten-shilling note and scrap of paper and stuffed them into a large black wallet. Bookmaking business over, he became a chargehand again. 'Right, you idle layabouts, back to the grindstone before old Fothersgill catches you loafing in here.'

As Eddie and I walked back to our workplace, I thought about the 'crazy' Australian. Perhaps he wasn't as crazy as they all thought. I decided that it was something I would check out, by following his selections to see if they ever came in.

*   *   *   *

On the tram next morning I borrowed Eddie's *Daily Mirror* and checked the racing results. 'Sydney's Pride' had *won* at 14 to one.

CHAPTER 21

▼

'Now, you know what you've got to do, Eddie, don't you?'

We were sitting on the tram, on our way to the docks, and I was briefing Eddie on what he was to do when I introduced my Crown and Anchor board to our fellow workers in the site restroom at lunchtime.

'Yes, of course I do. As soon as you lay the board out on the table, I come over and ask if I can play. You tell me to place my bet, or bets, on whatever I fancy; crowns, anchors, hearts, clubs, diamonds or spades. I place sixpence on the anchor and you shake the three dice and plop them down with the cup over them, lift the cup and shout, "Three anchors, you've won one and sixpence." By this time an audience should be gathering in the hut. You pay me out and ask if I want another go. I say, "No, I'm quitting while I'm ahead" and go and sit down to read my *Daily Mirror.*'

'That's terrific, Eddie, you've got the whole act off perfectly. Just one point though—when you're reading your paper sit by the window and keep an eye out for any of the foremen or chargehands, especially old Fothersgill. If one should show up give me a quick nudge and I'll fold up the board and put it under the table.'

Arriving at the docks I put the Crown and Anchor board and a leather dice cup in my canvas bag and hung it up under my raincoat, in the restroom.

I wished away the time to lunchtime, hoping it would rain for if it did I knew that most of the workers—my potential punters—would remain in the hut, rather than walk to the local shops and pubs, or play football on the waste ground around the hut. I had gathered all the loose change, pennies, threepenny bits and sixpences, I could scrounge from my mother, Eddie and Dennis, with the promise that I would pay them back with interest at the end of the week.

Eddie and I were first into the restroom at lunchtime. I quickly ate my sandwiches before anyone else arrived. The men began to drift in a few minutes later and when there were about a dozen in the hut, I opened the board and laid it on the table. Eddie joined me and played his part to perfection. Immediate interest was aroused and several men crowded around the board. I quickly explained the simple rules, for the benefit of those who had not played the game before, and we started in earnest. As I suspected, most of the men bet only in pennies. The odds always being in the banker's favour, I was winning, and my pile of pennies was growing by the minute.

We all became so wrapped up with the simple excitement of the game that none of us realised how fast our hour's lunch break was slipping away. Suddenly Eddie leaned forwards in his chair and banged my leg with his fist. Bolsover, the bricklayers' foreman, was on his way to the hut. Foremen rarely shared the restroom with the workers, preferring to take their breaks in the site foreman's office. This foreman was probably coming to give instructions to one of his gang, or, more likely, had been told by the site foreman to chase us all back to work. I quickly cleared the money off the board and put it and the three dice in an empty pocket. I closed the board and slipped it under the table.

As the foreman entered the men arose from their seats, put their belongings away and made to go back to their work. Eddie left, but I felt that I would have to stay to put the Crown and Anchor board in my canvass bag before it was discovered by one of the supervisory staff. The foreman noted my reluctance to leave. 'What's wrong with you, Archie, got lead in your pants?'

'No, Mr Bolsover, I'm on my way,' I said, as I scuttled out of the door.

I needn't have worried, as the board was still where I had left it when we went to the hut for our afternoon break.

*   *   *   *

The Crown and Anchor game proved to be a roaring success. More and more of the workmen joined in and after three or four weeks it had become an established practice for most of them to take part. We had a couple of scares, but Eddie always managed to warn me if any of the supervisors were approaching the hut. The players' stakes gradually got higher and it was now nothing for them to bet as much as a shilling— the limit I had set. Many won and went away happy, others were down on the day, but were always ready to return to try to win back their losses. My winnings were growing rapidly, affording me a grander life-style. I took Felicity out more often, was able to buy myself some much-needed clothing, and indulged myself with more expensive cigarettes and visits to the local pubs.

The game had been running for a couple of months, when I suddenly realised that I only had about two or three weeks of freedom before I had to report to RAF Padgate to start my national service. I needed to make the most of the time I had left to profit from the Crown and Anchor game. I raised the limit from one shilling to half a crown, which tempted a few of the players to make higher bets.

*   *   *   *

One Friday session, when players were crowding around the board and betting briskly, Eddie lightly kicked my shin. I immediately called a halt to the game and was about to return the stake money, before putting the board away, when Ozzie, who was sitting near the window, called out softly: 'Play on, Archie, it's only that bloody mongrel, Mallick. He daren't report us for gambling when he works as a tout for a bloody bookmaker!'

Others agreed. 'Play on, play on!' they cried.

Mallick walked into the room. 'What's all this then? Oh, I see,' he went on, as he neared the table, 'you're playing Crown and Anchor. I haven't played that since I left the army. Do you mind if I join in, Archie?'

'Not at all, Mr Mallick, you're welcome to join in. The upper limit for bets is a half-crown.'

Mallick rummaged in his trousers pocket, produced a half-crown, then placed it on the ace of spades. I waited a minute or two for the players to place their bets, but none did, probably being more interested in what the unpopular Mallick was doing. I shook the dice and released them from the cup.

'Club, diamond and anchor,' I called out, and picked up Mallick's half-crown.

Mallick scowled, but said nothing as he produced two more half-crowns. He placed one on the anchor and one on the ace of hearts.

'You're betting more than a half-crown,' I objected.

'No, I'm not; I'm betting on two squares and keeping within your limit on each of them. Are you sure you know what you're doing? There are rules to this game and you can't tell me anything about this game that I don't know already. I was playing it when you were cutting your milk teeth.'

'Very well, I shall accept your bets,' I replied, as I shook the dice and released them from the cup. 'Two anchors and one diamond,' I called out, as I raked in Mallick's two half-crowns.

Interest from the dozen or more spectators suddenly grew and some pushed forwards to get nearer the board as Mallick kept betting half-crowns. He continued to lose and, after exhausting his supply of coins, handed me a pound note to retrieve the eight he had lost. The keen players started to place bets, always avoiding the squares that Mallick had selected.

Mallick ran out of coins again and paused from play, while he examined the contents of his wallet. Turning to me he said: 'OK, that's enough for today. Anyway, it's time you lot were back at work.'

No one argued, least of all me. I was up about three pounds on the session and wanted to keep the game going until I left the firm.

*   *   *   *

During the days that followed, Mallick always joined in the game. He said little to his fellow workers and they had little to do with him, unless they wanted to place a bet on a horse or greyhound. It seemed to me that he was glad that the men, who were always ready to have a 'flutter' on the horses, were assembled at a convenient spot and in the mood to gamble.

Mallick's luck changed and he started to break about even after most sessions. My regular punters supported the game and continued to make consistent, but modest, bets, their losses enabling me to continue to enjoy the benefits I was fast taking for granted.

I met my *Waterloo* a few days before the 1948 Grand National. The restroom was filled to capacity with Crown and Anchor players and

Mallick was taking bets faster than a London bus conductor could take fares. When they were not placing Grand National bets with Mallick the company played at my game. I was happy the money was steadily coming my way.

Mallick joined the crowd around the board and placed a half-crown on the anchor, the ace of clubs and the ace of diamonds. All the other players followed their usual practice of avoiding Mallick's selections and placed their shilling and sixpenny bets on the vacant ace of hearts, ace of clubs and the crown. I shook the dice vigorously and tipped them from the cup.

'Anchor, club and diamond win,' I called, nearly choking when I realised that Mallick had accurately forecast three of the six squares.

I paid him out and cleared the sixpences and shillings from the board. Mallick repeated his success with his next bets on the crown, ace of hearts and ace of clubs. The shilling and sixpenny punters went down again. This was disastrous for me; I was paying out half-crowns and taking in shillings and sixpences.

Mallick said nothing, but his smug expression told me everything. He was out to get me and if the other players continued losing their modest stakes, and Mallick's luck held out with his half-crown bets, he could break my bank. I prayed that something would happen to stop the game before I was completely cleaned out. Something did happen. Eddie, who had been sitting quietly in a vacant corner of the room, reading his newspaper, but hearing what was going on at the table, suddenly let out a cry, slid off his chair and lay motionless on the floor. I immediately stopped play, pushed my way through the crowded room and knelt at his side. He appeared to be struggling for breath so I loosened his collar and cradled his head in my hands.

'Open the bloody door and windows!' I shouted. 'There's no air in here. Eddie has fainted because it's so stuffy.'

Everyone rushed to comply and in a few seconds Eddie opened his eyes and gave me a sly wink. The artful old sod must have heard my silent prayer and created the diversion to stop the game. By the time Eddie had 'recovered' from his false fainting spell, most of the players had left to return to work. Mallick and Ozzie remained behind.

'Jack, will you put this pony on "Sheila's Cottage" to win The Grand National for me?' asked Ozzie, handing Mallick a sheaf of new pound notes.

'Did I hear you right, Ozzie? I can't believe you want to put 25 pounds on "Sheila's Cottage"; it's a rank outsider and will probably start at about 66 to one,' said Mallick, scornfully.

'Yes, Jacko, that's exactly what I want to do. Remember, I always favour the outsiders. Just imagine if this one came in, I'd be about 1,650 pounds richer.'

'Well, it's *your* money and it's not for me to put people off their selections; after all, the bookmaker pays me commission on all the bets I collect for him. If your bet goes down he'll probably give me a bonus.'

I had been counting what money I had left and replacing my board in my canvas bag, but had been paying great attention to their conversation.

Mallick turned to me. 'There's still about 15 minutes of our lunch break left, so why don't you get the board out for a few more shakes of the dice? I'm sure Ozzie would like to play a bit longer.'

'Sure thing, I'm game,' said Ozzie with a laugh.

I knew I should refuse, but there was always the chance that Mallick's luck would change again and he would start losing, enabling me to recover some of my losses. 'Righto, Mr Mallick, we've just got time for about five shakes of the dice,' I said, as I placed the board on the table and put the three dice in the cup.

'Shall we raise the limit, Archie? What about making it a ten-shilling limit? We'd be playing with paper money then,' said Mallick.

'That's OK by me,' said Ozzie.

Well, I thought, I can't afford to lose, but my luck has got to change.

'The new limit is ten-shillings. Place your bets, gentlemen.'

Mallick played his three squares, a ten-shilling note on each. Ozzie bet a half-crown on the anchor. Mallick's selections all came up. Three throws later I was completely busted, with not enough money left to fully pay out Mallick and Ozzie, who had been betting on the same squares as Mallick.

'I'm afraid that's it, gents. You've broken the bank. The game is over, for good. I'll have to owe you 30 bob, Jack. I've just got enough to pay Ozzie his five bob winnings from the last throw.'

'Well, tomorrow is pay day, so you can let me have my money then,' said Mallick with a wolfish grin.

'You can forget mine, kiddo. It was fun playing and winning, but I wouldn't want you to go home stony broke,' said Ozzie with a wide grin.

'Don't encourage him, Ozzie. He should pay for his mistakes. I've done him a favour by busting him. It's been a good lesson for him and perhaps next time he won't be so cocksure of himself—and you two can get back to work now,' Mallick added, as he walked out of the hut.

Ozzie and I walked back to our respective work sites. As we were about to go our separate ways, I asked: 'Why did you pick "Sheila's Cottage" to win The Grand National, Ozzie? I know why you picked that winning long shot, "Sydney's Pride"—it was because you come from Sydney, wasn't it?'

'Well, I'll be damned! You've worked out my system of betting. The simple fact is that I only bet on horses that have some connection with

Australia. I guess I must be a lucky buck because I win more than I lose.'

'But why, "Sheila's Cottage"?'

'Because in Australia girls are called 'sheilas', and my sheila, or rather my wife, Kerry, a real hard worker with a well-paid job, has just bought us a cottage on the coast, just south of Sydney. I've been working here since the war and been doing plenty of overtime, so I was able to send a lot of cash back to Oz to help pay for the cottage. So, you see, Archie, I am a lucky cuss. Everything seems to go my way.'

'That's great, Ozzie, I hope things stay that way for you. I shan't be here much longer as I'm going into the RAF to do my national service, but I'll not forget you, and every time I see that a horse connected with Australia wins a race I'll think of you. Cheerio, Ozzie,' I called out, as I walked away to join Eddie at our work site.

'Oh, so you are going to do some work today. I was beginning to think that you'd buggered off home, but of course, you wouldn't do that on a pay day, would you?' said Eddie with a grin, which told me that he was only giving me a mild rebuke. It took a lot to make Eddie angry about anything, but an apology did seem in order.

'I'm sorry, Eddie; I got talking to Ozzie and forgot the time.'

'Yes, I know, Ozzie can spin a great yarn. If they had a "telling tall stories" event in the Olympics this summer, he'd be the boyo to represent Australia, but if I were you I wouldn't take too much notice of his tales. He's inclined to exaggerate his skill at playing the horses. When it comes to backing winners, I think he's just one of life's lucky buggers.'

I nodded agreement, but thought differently—I'd already made up my mind to see if I could share some of Ozzie's luck.

*   *   *   *

As soon as Fothersgill's clerk handed me my pay packet I took Mallick the money I owed him. He took it without a word of thanks and stuffed it into his wallet.

'Do you want to place a bet on the big race?' he called after me.

'No thanks, not with *you*, Mr Mallick,' I retorted.

I had just two pounds left from my pay and I knew what I was going to do with one of those pounds.

*   *   *   *

On the way home that evening with Eddie, I asked him where I might place a bet on The Grand National.

'What, you betting on horses, that's something new for you. Anyway, after Mallick cleaning you out on the Crown and Anchor, I'd have thought you'd have little money left to play the horses.'

'I know, but it's something I want to do, and I'll not be talked out of it by anyone.'

'OK, then we'll call in at The Salutation for a pint. John McCafferty is your man. He practically lives in the pub and will take bets from anybody, and he'll not cheat you. In fact he's noted for his honest dealings. Some punters call him 'Honest' John. What do you fancy, then?'

'"*Sheila's Cottage*" to win.'

'"*Sheila's Cottage*" gasped Eddie, 'that donkey could only win if it went around the course just once. Don't waste your money on it.'

'It's "Sheila's Cottage", or nothing,' I snapped back.

'All right, all right, it's your money, but I hope you've enough left for your mother's housekeeping allowance.'

'She'll not go short on account of me gambling, even if I have to pawn my best suit.'

We entered The Salutation and Eddie immediately pointed out John, who was standing at the end of the bar with a pint of Guinness in his left hand.

'Hello, John, and how do we find you today?' greeted Eddie, as we joined him at the bar.

'I'm as fine as can be expected. How are you, Eddie?'

'Oh, I can't complain, and it wouldn't make a ha'p'orth of difference if I did. This young man is my stepson, Archie. He's not been in here before.'

I shook hands with John.

'He's got a good handshake, Eddie. I like and trust a man with a strong handshake. What'll you both have to drink?' asked John.

'Oh, no, this round is on me. Finish that pint, John, and there'll be another waiting for you,' said Eddie as he turned to the barman to order the three drinks.

'We came in hoping to see you here, John. Archie wants to make a bet on The Grand National, and I recommended that he place it with you.'

'Yes, indeed, I'm your man if you want to place a bet,' said John, as he drained his glass. 'What do you fancy, Archie?'

'"*Sheila's Cottage*". I'd like to put a pound on it to win.'

'"*Sheila's Cottage*"—bejabbers, I shouldn't be saying this to a punter, but since you're Eddie's son, and Eddie's a great mate of mine, I have to tell you that horse has no chance at all. It's a rank outsider. Don't throw your money away on it. Back any other horse in the race, or better still, save your money. Gambling's a mug's game. Take it from someone who makes his living from it.'

'Thanks for the good advice, John, but that's my choice and I'm sticking to it,' I said, as I handed him a pound note.

McCafferty took a bulging wallet and a black notebook from his donkey jacket pocket. He carefully placed the banknote in the wallet, wrote something in his notebook and handed me a slip of paper.

'Right, Archie, you're on *"Sheila's Cottage"* to win, with odds of 50 to one.'

We stayed talking to John long enough for him to finish his Guinness and Eddie to buy another round of drinks, and then went home.

*   *   *   *

It was Saturday, 4th April, the day of the 1948 Grand National; I could hardly contain myself. I stayed in all morning, reading the various sports writers' predictions of which horse would win, searching for anything that was written about my selection. The only information I found was that '*Sheila's Cottage*' was owned by Harry Lane, trained by Neville Crump and was to be ridden by Arthur Thompson. The starting price was given as 50 to one. I prayed that Arthur had had a good breakfast that morning and that the horse was in fine form.

A few minutes before the race was due to start, Eddie joined me in the sitting room to listen to the radio commentary. We listened intently to the second by second commentary describing the positions of the leading horses and the names of those that fell at the various jumps. After about five minutes I could bear it no longer; the tension was too great. I went into the kitchen to make a pot of tea and as I poured the boiling water into the teapot I heard Eddie shouting from the sitting room.

'You've won, Archie, you've won! *"Sheila's Cottage"* has come in first. Come back in here.'

I dashed back into the sitting room, nearly dropping the laden tea tray in my haste.

'Never mind tea, *this* calls for a real drink!' Eddie cried out with delight. 'We'll open that bottle of 12-year-old malt I've been saving, as soon as your mother gets in from her shopping.'

Eddie and I went to The Salutation that evening to collect my winnings. John McCafferty was standing at the bar, where we had last seen him, with a pint of Guinness in his left hand. He was in a very good mood. No wonder, the favourites had fallen and he had little to pay out.

'You're the only one I know who backed "*Sheila's Cottage*",' he said, as he passed me a thick roll of pound notes, held together with an elastic band. 'You've no need to count them. You'll find that the money is all there, including your stake money.'

'I'm sure you're right, John, and thank you,' I said, as I peeled a pound note from the roll and slipped it into his hand.

'Thanks, Archie,' said John as he slapped the pound note on the bar and called out to the barman, 'the same again please and one for yourself.'

We stayed talking with John McCafferty for about an hour and I bought another round of drinks. By the time they had been drunk I was beginning to feel a bit woozy.

'I think we ought to call it a day, John,' said Eddie, as he grabbed my shoulder to prevent me slipping off my barstool.

'Yes, Eddie, I'm sure you're right. Best get the lad home and into bed. He's had enough excitement, not to mention beer, for one day. Goodnight, Eddie.'

'Goodnight, John, be seeing you,' replied Eddie, as he helped me across the crowded bar floor to the door. I turned as we neared the pub door and gave John a weary wave.

Before catching a bus home, Eddie stopped at the mobile coffee stall in the town square and ordered two strong coffees. 'We must get you livened up a bit before we get home. Your mother will have a fit if she sees you in this state.'

I felt better after two cups of strong coffee and the fresh night air helped clear my head. On the bus home I kept my right hand in my jacket pocket, holding the thick roll of banknotes and thinking about what I could buy. I'd get a very special present for my mother and take a bouquet of spring flowers to my grandmother. She'd like that. She had no flowers in her tiny back garden, only onions and runner beans, and she rarely received flowers from any of her family. Eddie was easy; I knew he wanted a new tool bag. I'd get my grandfather a briar pipe. Cyril would be happy with a book or a blowout at Manzies eel and pie shop, but what could I get for Felicity? It had to be something special; something that she would really appreciate. I didn't care how much it cost as I could afford it. I'd sleep on the problem and hope to come up with an answer before Monday, when I planned to make my farewells to Felicity and her parents.

When we arrived home I said a hasty 'Goodnight' to my mother and Eddie, and went to my room. I thought I'd soon be asleep, but I wasn't; the thought of the bundle of pound notes, now in my bedside locker drawer, kept me awake for hours.

*   *   *   *

'Mum, if you could have anything you wanted for the house, what would you choose?' I asked, as I spread beef dripping on my breakfast toast.

My mother looked at me questioningly. 'What are you on about, Archie?'

'You know I won a tidy sum on The Grand National; well, I want to buy you something special. Something you really want. Something just for you.'

'I should have to give that some very careful thought, son, but you don't want to go splashing your winnings about. Save your money for something worthwhile. You've always wanted a modern portable type-writer so why don't you buy yourself one of those?'

'Yes, Mum, I probably will, but I still want to buy you something special.'

My mother smiled. 'All right, Archie, if it would really please you to buy me a present, I'd like it to be something that would be of benefit to us all. After last year's terrible winter and the coal rationing, it would be good to have an oil-fired heater, one of those new Valor oil stoves, to help warm up this draughty old house. They are supposed to be quite safe and cheap to run and we've got an oil shop at the top of the road, so we need never be out of fuel.'

'Very well, Mum, an oil stove you shall have. I'll get one tomorrow.'

I spent the rest of the day making a list of my family and friends, and the presents I would buy them. By the time I had finished I found that I would not have enough money to buy all the things that I had planned. I'd have to give up the idea of buying the new typewriter. Never mind, I'd probably not have much time to use one in the RAF and, anyway, I needed to save enough money to take my mother and Eddie out for a farewell drink at the local pub.

*   *   *   *

'Good evening, Mrs Farnley, these are for you,' I said, handing her a large bunch of spring flowers. 'Is Felicity in?'

'Yes, Archie, she's in and waiting for you. Thank you for the flowers. They're lovely; how kind of you,' Mrs Farnley said as she stepped aside to let me into the hall.

Mrs Farnley ushered me into the sitting room, where I found Felicity on her own, sitting on the settee reading a dog-eared copy of *The Tatler*.

'I'll leave you two lovebirds on your own, and go and put these lovely flowers in water,' said Mrs Farnley, with an almost silent giggle as she left the room.

'Hello, Felicity, my darling,' I said, and as she arose from the settee, kissed her on the cheek. 'I came over to say goodbye, or as you students of French would say, *au revoir*, because it'll only be two or three months before I get my first home leave. I also came to bring you this token of my love for you,' I said, as I took a small jewellery box from my coat pocket and handed it to her.

Felicity, her eyes shining and her cheeks glowing with pleasure, opened the box.

'Oh, it's a gold locket and chain,' she said with surprise, opening the locket. 'And it has a picture of you in it. I do believe it's your head cut from the photograph my father took of us in the back garden, when you first came to this house. What a wonderful surprise. How thoughtful of you to buy me such a delightful gift. I shall always wear it.'

Felicity put the locket chain around her neck and moved towards me, her arms outstretched. 'Oh, rascal that you are, I do adore you, Archie.'

I clasped her in my arms and kissed her passionately on the lips.

When we pulled apart almost breathless, I said, 'It's a lovely evening, so why don't we go out for a nice walk, to somewhere romantic, where we can talk about our future together?'

Felicity gave me the most seductive look I'd ever seen on any girl's face and replied, 'Why ever not, my darling Archie.'

CHAPTER 22

▼

Well, I've arrived well before time and there doesn't seem to be any other new recruits around, I thought, as I approached the building bearing the title, 'Main Guardroom', at the entrance to RAF Padgate. I walked up to the glass-fronted hatch and a corporal appeared. He looked at me as if I had just crawled out from under a stone.

'New recruits, report to the reception centre, 200 yards down the road on the left,' he shouted at me.

I didn't reply, but turned and walked in the direction he had pointed. Entering the building, I found myself in a huge room. A corporal sat at a large desk at the other side of the room. He saw me standing in the entrance and beckoned me to his desk. I started to walk across the vast expanse of highly polished wood floor, but I had barely taken two steps when the corporal leapt to his feet and screamed: 'Get off that floor, you horrible little man! It's not for walking on. Can't you see the marked walking area around the room?'

I retreated and walked around to the narrow strip of floor space, which was marked out with white paint, and stood in front of his desk. 'I'm sorry about walking on your nice shiny floor, but I have always been led to believe that the shortest distance between two points was a straight line.'

That was a mistake—the corporal turned a purple hue.

'Oh, so you're a wise guy, eh? Carry on like that when you're doing your basic training and you'll find yourself in deep shit! What's your name?' he asked, his pencil poised over a sheaf of papers on his desk.

'Cholmondeley, Archibald Sinclair Cholmondeley,' I replied in a loud voice.

'Well, Cholmondeley,' snarled the corporal, 'you can wait outside on the road for the rest of the shower of new recruits that are expected to arrived today.' He made the word 'recruits' sound like an obscenity.

I didn't reply. I knew it would be a mistake to utter the words that came readily to my mind, and simply turned on my heels and marched, with an exaggerated swagger, back down the narrow strip of floor, upon which new recruits were permitted to tread.

Standing on the road outside the reception centre, I wondered what would be in store for me during the next two years. Not much prospect of making any money. I'd heard that national servicemen were paid only four shillings a day and a lot of that had to be spent on metal polish, boot polish and blanco, whatever that was. Not to worry. I'd have to take things as they came. I'd always managed to find some way or other to supplement my income. Perhaps I could flog some RAF kit and equipment. Those Army and Navy stores had to get their gear from somewhere, so why not from me? Why should things be any different in the Royal Air Force? That they *were* very different was something I was soon to find out, but that's another story…

About the Author

Bryan Marlowe was born in Holborn, City of London, 1930. Attended 22 schools, leaving at the age of 14. Had numerous jobs before National Service in the Royal Air Force—1948/50. Rejoined the RAF in 1951 and retired in 1971. Worked for 20 years with a northern police force. On retirement took up voluntary work with Victim and Witness Support and worked as newspaper columnist. Has extensively travelled the five continents and lived abroad.

More information at www.diadembooks.com/marlowe.htm

978-0-595-38830-1
0-595-38830-2

Lightning Source UK Ltd.
Milton Keynes UK
UKOW052101150612

194487UK00001B/190/A